"How Long Have We Been Married?"

Lauren asked softly.

He turned his head so that he was staring into her eyes. "I don't know. How long would you like to have been married?"

"Maybe three years? That would give us time to be used to each other, don't you think?"

"I have no idea. Three years is as good as any, I suppose."

"Do we have any children?"

"No!" he answered abruptly.

"You don't want them?"

"Why are you asking all of these ridiculous questions, Lauren?"

"I enjoy the challenge of working out a puzzle."

"Well, I'm not a puzzle that you have to figure out."

No doubt he was right. They weren't going to be together long enough for her to need to understand the type of person he was. However, for some reason that she couldn't quite fathom, she wanted to get back in touch with the laughing man she'd caught a glimpse of earlier.

Her insatiable curiosity had once again taken over.

Dear Reader:

Welcome! You hold in your hand a Silhouette Desire—your ticket to a whole new world of reading pleasure.

A Silhouette Desire is a sensuous, contemporary romance about passions, problems and the ultimate power of love. It is about today's woman—intelligent, successful, giving—but it is also the story of a romance between two people who are strong enough to follow their own individual paths, yet strong enough to compromise, as well.

These books are written by, for and about every woman that you are—wife, mother, sister, lover, daughter, career woman. A Silhouette Desire heroine must face the same challenges, achieve the same successes, in her story as you do in your own life.

The Silhouette reader is not afraid to enjoy herself. She knows when to take things seriously and when to indulge in a fantasy world. With six books a month, Silhouette Desire strives to meet her many moods, but each book is always a compelling love story.

Make a commitment to romance—go wild with Silhouette Desire!

Best,

Isabel Swift
Senior Editor & Editorial Coordinator

ANNETTE BROADRICK
Momentary Marriage

Silhouette Desire

Published by Silhouette Books New York

America's Publisher of Contemporary Romance

SILHOUETTE BOOKS
300 East 42nd St., New York, N.Y. 10017

Copyright © 1988 by Annette Broadrick

ISBN: 0-373-05414-9

First Silhouette Books printing March 1988

America's Publisher of Contemporary Romance

Printed in the U.S.A.

ANNETTE BROADRICK

lives on the shores of The Lake of the Ozarks in Missouri, where she spends her time doing what she loves most—reading and writing romance fiction. "For twenty-five years I lived in various large cities, working as a legal secretary, a very high-stress occupation. I never thought I was capable of making a career change at this point in my life, but thanks to Silhouette I am now able to write full-time in the peaceful surroundings that have turned my life into a dream come true."

This book is dedicated to the many friends I've made at The Lake of the Ozarks. You have welcomed me into your homes and hearts as though I were part of the family.

Thank you, dear friends. You are part of my heart, also.

One

As he rapidly strode down the long hallway to Mallory's office, Jordan Trent watched, with a certain amount of grim humor, a couple of staff members as they scattered before him like quail in the presence of a hunting dog. Mallory had gone too far this time. Jordan intended to tell him exactly what he thought of him and his damned emergencies. Jordan was sick to death of the constant pressure and unremitting tension of his job. He had needed every minute of his vacation, something that Mallory didn't seem to understand.

How dare Mallory pull this latest stunt! Jordan fully intended that someone would pay for this. From the reactions of those with whom he'd come into contact since he'd arrived at the office, it was obvious to Jordan that his mood had communicated itself to those around him.

He barely slowed his pace when he reached the correct office. Grabbing the knob of the unmarked door, Jordan thrust the door open and walked in without bothering to knock. James Mallory glanced up without surprise from the papers he was holding. In fact, Mallory's expression showed no emotion at all.

Jordan hadn't expected anything else.

Mallory never gave his thoughts away and as far as Jordan could prove, Mallory didn't possess any emotions.

Without waiting for an invitation, Jordan sank into the well-padded chair in front of the scarred desk and said, "This had better be good," in a menacing tone.

Mallory leaned back in his chair and met the implacable gaze of the man across the desk from him. "So how was your vacation, J.D.?"

"Funny you should ask. What the hell was so all-fired important that it couldn't have waited another week?"

Mallory studied the younger man in silence for a few minutes. "Somehow I thought having time off would help to sweeten your disposition." He shrugged. "I can't really expect to be right a hundred percent of the time, I suppose."

"I don't need your harassment, Mallory. Why did you level your artillery at me?"

Mallory raised his bushy brows slightly. "Artillery?"

"You know damned well what I mean. Telling the local police I was wanted back in the States!"

"You are," Mallory responded mildly.

"Your implication was that I am highly dangerous."

"You are," he added with a nod.

"And that I am wanted by the government . . . 'you are,'" he mimicked along with Mallory as the other man agreed with the statement. "Dammit, Mallory! Your so-called sense of humor definitely needs an adjustment or two."

"Are you saying I ruined your image on, uh— what's the name of that island you were visiting?"

"It doesn't matter. I suddenly found myself persona non grata and was asked to leave. Immediately."

Mallory shrugged. "You ignored my messages."

"Why shouldn't I have? This was my first vacation in five years. Five years, Mallory. I know damned well I'm not the only operative you've got working for you. So why me?"

"I need your special skills on this one."

"What special skills? My rare ability to keep myself from getting killed?"

Mallory nodded. "There is that. Plus you have the unusual ability of always getting what you're after. We need that little extra boost on this one, I'm afraid."

"I'm touched, Mallory. I really am. How long have I worked for you now? Eight—ten years? And I do believe I've just heard the first compliment you've ever paid—to me or to anyone. Do you suppose you could repeat it for taping? You know, as a little token to remind me of you in the unlikely event I should ever allow your presence to slip from my mind."

Mallory leaned back in his chair and put his feet up on the desk. He stared at the younger man for a moment with pursed lips. "Of course," he admitted wryly, "you do have a way of ignoring all the procedural guidelines that have been handed down from above, which has created something of a furor from time to time."

"So fire me," Jordan suggested in a hard tone.

"You're too eager," Mallory pointed out quietly.

"You're right about that. I'm too old for this kind of life, Mallory. I've been telling you that for the past two years."

"So you have. But you don't really mean it and we both know it. You thrive on living on the edge, surviving by your wits and instincts." He paused and lit a cigarette. "Face it, J.D.," he said, exhaling a lungful of smoke, "You'd be bored with any other life."

Jordan waved the smoke away in disgust. "Thank you, Dr. Mallory. And how much do I owe you for this vocational counseling session?"

Mallory allowed himself a small smile. "Just one of the fringe benefits around here. I don't even require a fee."

"Good thing. Do you have any idea what my plane fare to get halfway around the world from you set me back? And it still wasn't far enough!"

"I'll see that you're reimbursed."

Mallory's quiet tone caused Jordan to study him for a moment in silence. "This deal must really be important," Jordan finally said. "I've never seen you willing to part with any cash before."

Mallory met his gaze with an implacable expression. "I really need you on this one."

"Which one is that—?"

"Does the name Trevor Monroe mean anything to you?"

"Of course. He's the U.S. senator from Virginia."

"And heads up the Senate Overseas Intelligence Committee."

"Are we being investigated?" Jordan asked facetiously. "Again?"

"No. We've been given permission to pull out all the stops on this one."

"I'm afraid to even ask," Jordan said slowly. He hadn't heard that tone of voice from Mallory before. Whatever it was that was in the works, it was serious.

"The senator's wife has been having some health problems. He decided to take her to see a specialist in Vienna. Very few people knew about this trip, for obvious reasons. The senator is in a very sensitive position with our government."

"So what does he want—surveillance? A guard? Should I pretend to be his wife's brother?"

"Too bad we didn't think of that earlier. You see, Frances Monroe disappeared two days ago while en route to the doctor's clinic for tests."

Jordan immediately understood the implications: holding a member of a government official's family automatically insured that official's full cooperation.

"Do they have any idea who did it?"

"None. We've kept it quiet and no one has come forward claiming responsibility."

"Where's the leak in security?"

Mallory realized that Jordan had already dismissed his ire at his forced return. Jordan recognized that the government had a serious problem that could reach catastrophic proportions if not handled properly.

"We're working on it. In the meantime, it's an all-out hunt to find Mrs. Monroe."

"Where do I come in?"

"We think she was taken behind the iron curtain—either into Czechoslovakia or Hungary. You know that area better than anyone we have and you've got contacts there. We're counting on you to get her out."

"You never ask for much, do you, Mallory?" Jordan asked, disgust evident in his tone. He shook his head and stretched his legs out in front of him, crossing them at the ankles.

"I know you prefer to work alone—" Mallory began.

"*Insist* on working alone," Jordan inserted smoothly, studying the shine of his shoes with considerable interest.

"Yes. Well, whatever. This is going to take two of you."

Jordan straightened slightly, his gaze lifting slowly until it met Mallory's eyes. "No exceptions, Mallory."

"I can understand your feelings, J.D. Particularly after what happened in Istanbul last year."

"My so-called backup almost got me killed."

"An unfortunate incident."

"It would have been even more unfortunate...at least to me...if he'd succeeded."

"You have no need to worry about loyalty this time. Your assistant can be counted on to be there for you."

"Thanks, but I'm not interested." Jordan kept his eyes trained on the man who was nominally his boss, wishing he could gain some insight into the man's thinking processes.

After the incident in Istanbul, Jordan had tried to get Mallory to fire him—right after Mallory had tossed Jordan's written resignation into the wastebasket with no more than a glance.

At that meeting, Jordan had learned a great deal about the agency for which he worked. His was a lifetime job. Unfortunately, the statistics for his line of work didn't give him too many years to worry about.

"Why don't you let me catch a flight to Vienna this evening, Mallory, and we'll see what I can come up with? If I need reinforcement, believe me, I'll contact you immediately."

"It isn't that simple."

"I never pretended it would be simple. But if you want me to meet with my contacts, I need to do it alone."

"That's all right, she won't be—"

"She? What are you talking about, *she*, Mallory? We don't have any female operatives."

"Lauren isn't exactly an operative, although she does work in one of the departments here."

Jordan stood and began to pace back and forth between the desk and the window. "Are you out of your mind, Mallory? You expect me to take an amateur with me?"

"Lauren is in our cryptology department. She's a very bright lady—a mathematical whiz that we recruited right out of college. She's also multilingual."

Jordan, his hands on his hips, stopped pacing and glared at Mallory. "I don't care if she pole vaults, sings "God Bless America" while standing on her head and placed in the Olympics, I don't want her."

"You have no choice. The senator insists we have a woman there for his wife. He feels his wife will need that added emotional support."

Jordan began pacing again. "I don't believe this. I simply don't believe it. You want me to perform a damn miracle and now you throw in a sizable handicap and tell me I have no choice."

Mallory didn't look at Jordan. Instead he leaned over and punched a button on his phone. When a disembodied voice answered, he said, "Please ask Ms. Mackenzie to come in." He brought his feet down from the desk and folded his hands in front of him.

"Why would an untrained woman want to get involved in this situation, Mallory? We don't have any idea what we're going to find over there. Just give me a chance to check things out—"

"We don't have time," Mallory stated in a firm tone. "You and Lauren are booked on an evening flight. Her passport states that she is your wife."

Jordan felt as though he'd either lost his hearing or his sanity. He wasn't sure which loss would be easier to accept. "My wife?" he repeated, almost in a whisper.

Mallory nodded. "There're fewer complications that way."

Jordan walked over to the window and adjusted the blind so that he could peer out. Yes, the familiar landscape reassured him that most of his senses were still functioning adequately. He glanced over his shoulder. "I don't know the first thing about wives or having one. I certainly don't see how having a strange woman along as a wife would make things less complicated."

"Because you're going to have to spend all your time together, except when you need to reach your contacts. Then Lauren will be the typical American wife who enjoys shopping while her husband is busy with business."

"How is it you make your explanations sound so reasonable when I know that the whole scheme is totally insane?"

There was a knock on the door. Instead of answering Jordan, Mallory raised his voice slightly and said, "Come in."

Jordan watched from his position by the window as a young woman opened the door and walked into the room. Then he realized the whole thing must be a joke. She looked like a caricature of a prim, brainy, introverted and totally repressed professional woman. No one dressed that way any more.

Granted Jordan didn't know all that much about women's styles, either in hairdos or business suits, but this woman gave the impression that she was interested in neither. She wore a two-piece suit that effectively concealed her figure. She could be Twiggy-thin or in the late stages of a pregnancy, for all he could tell by the clothes she wore. Her hair was haphazardly pulled to the nape of her neck in a loose coil. Several wisps had come loose and fell in front of her ears and along her neck.

The tortoiseshell glasses and the low-heeled sensible shoes reminded Jordan of *Marian the Librarian*, a character from a play he'd seen in college.

Mallory's sense of humor had always been a little bizarre, but Jordan thought he'd carried the joke to an extreme this time, seemingly insensitive to this woman's feelings.

Jordan watched as she walked over to Mallory's desk without glancing toward the window. She spoke to Mallory in a low well-modulated voice.

"You wished to see me, Mr. Mallory?"

"Yes, Lauren. Please have a seat." He nodded to one of the chairs across from him. "I want you to meet Jordan Trent. As I've previously explained, he's the man you'll be working with."

Jordan watched as the woman slowly turned her head and looked at him. She did not change her expression. "Mr. Trent," she murmured, nodding her head toward him. Then she sat down, crossed her legs and returned her gaze to Mallory.

Jordan had never felt quite so dismissed in his life and he found the sensation somewhat unsettling. She certainly hadn't seemed impressed with the man who supposedly was going to play an important role in her life for the next few days.

Not that he could take exception to her behavior. He certainly wasn't the embodiment of any woman's secret fantasies. He faced himself daily in the mirror and

knew that his harsh features, stern expression and
height were more intimidating than reassuring.

"Now that you two have had an opportunity to
meet," Mallory blandly stated, "I'd like to go over our
plans with you."

Jordan reluctantly returned to the chair he'd occupied earlier and sat down, which placed him next to
Lauren Mackenzie.

She glanced at him briefly and gave him a tentative
smile. If he hadn't been watching her so closely, he
would have missed it. A sudden thought flashed across
his mind. *She's shy!* Was that why she wore such an
effective camouflage, or had she in fact donned it for
his benefit? Whatever the reason, she certainly made
a statement.

"Now, then," Mallory began, glancing down at a
file in front of him. "Lauren fits the same general description as Mrs. Monroe. As soon as we're through
here she's going to have her hair restyled and lightened in order to more closely resemble Mrs. Monroe."

"Why?" Jordan demanded, not liking the sudden
suspicion that had crossed his mind.

"Because, if you succeed in finding Mrs. Monroe in
either Hungary or Czechoslovakia, she can leave the
country using Lauren's passport."

"You're making a few assumptions, aren't you,
Mallory?" Jordan asked. "We have no idea where
we're going to find Mrs. Monroe, or what her physical condition will be." He glanced around at Lauren.
"Why would you agree to voluntarily stay behind in a
potentially explosive situation?"

Lauren studied the irascible man beside her with something bordering on dismay. He was nothing like the person she had pictured when Mallory had first discussed the matter with her. Granted she rarely saw the men who reported to Mallory. She had assumed that the people working covert operations would be uniformly nondescript so that they could blend into their surroundings when necessary. There was no way this man could go anywhere unnoticed; she was confident of that.

He was several inches over six feet, with black, piercing eyes that seemed to stare a hole through her. His crisply curling hair glinted like a raven's wing in the light from the window. High cheekbones and a strong jawline completed the picture of a man no one in his right mind would choose to tangle with. He certainly wasn't the type of man who appealed to her at all.

Not that her personal preference had anything to do with the situation.

"I was told they needed someone of my general description. I was willing to help," she explained quietly.

Jordan shook his head. "You have no idea what you're getting into."

"Perhaps not. I suppose you'll have to explain it all to me as we go."

Was that sarcasm he heard in her quiet voice? He studied her more closely. Her calm, gray-eyed gaze met his without blinking.

"Do you have to wear those glasses?" Jordan asked abruptly. He was pleased to see that he had caught her off guard with his remark, then felt ashamed of himself for his reaction.

"Only for close work, Mr. Trent. However, much of what I do is close work."

"Well, you won't be doing any 'close' work on this trip. That should relieve your mind," he replied, his glance lazily going over her.

Lauren could feel the heat of temper filling her and, not for the first time, she wished that she had not inherited the temperament that seemed to plague redhaired people. His innuendo had been unnecessary and unjust. Did he think she had volunteered for the sake of spending time with him as his wife?

She reached up and pulled her glasses off. After methodically searching for the carrying case in her handbag, she placed the glasses in the case, the case in her purse, then looked at him again. "Is that better?"

Jordan found himself at a loss for words for a moment. Without the bulky frame of the glasses, he could see the beauty of her eyes. They were large and wideset, surrounded with a dark fringe of lashes that gave her gaze a mysterious depth. Her eyes continued to meet his without flinching. He coughed and nodded. "Uh, yes. I was just wondering. I mean..." He let the words trail away uncertainly. Where had he ever gotten the idea this woman was shy? From the look in her eyes and the soft flush in her cheeks, Jordan had the distinct impression he was not on her list of favorite people.

"Do you have any questions about all of this, J.D.?" Mallory asked.

"Questions, no. However, I have several objections." He turned in his chair so that he was facing Lauren more fully. "I don't have anything against you personally and I'm certainly not trying to discriminate because of your gender. But I am concerned about taking someone into the field with me who has no training. It's too dangerous. I don't need the extra worry." He turned back to Mallory. "Can't you appease the senator some way and give me a chance to see what I can do on my own?"

"No."

The immediate answer and the implacability of the tone put an end to that particular topic. After several moments of silence, Mallory said, "Anything else?"

Jordan prided himself on thinking fast on his feet and on his ability for getting himself out of tight situations. However, at that moment, he could see no way out of his dilemma. In his frustration, he muttered, "I don't have a clue how to pretend to be a husband."

Lauren kept her expression carefully noncommittal, although she could not prevent herself from softly biting down on her bottom lip to prevent a smile.

"I'm afraid we don't have time to give you a crash course in matrimony, J.D.," Mallory said with a grin.

"It isn't funny."

"I agree. This is deadly serious. All of it. However, I know you can handle it or I wouldn't have insisted on using you on this one." Mallory stood up, a clear indication that he considered the matter closed. "Do what you always do so well, J.D. Improvise."

Two

---

*I*mprovise, hell! Jordan thought furiously while packing for the trip a few hours later. He should have refused flat out. The whole idea was totally ridiculous. What did Mallory think he was pulling? Trying to do a little matchmaking? Maybe he hoped to find a man for his little cryptographer.

Well, it sure as hell wasn't going to be Jordan Trent. He was a loner and always had been. His life-style suited him perfectly. Mallory had been right about that—Jordan enjoyed what he did to make a living. He liked never knowing where he'd be the next week. He preferred the excitement and danger of his present life-style to the monotony of a nine-to-five existence, a house in the suburbs, a wife and children.

So why was he upset? This was going to be a tough assignment but he already knew several people who might be able to shed some light on the mysterious disappearance of Mrs. Monroe.

Jordan forced himself to face what was really eating at him. He didn't relate well to other people. He never had. Consequently, he'd never shared long periods of time with another person, male or female. The pattern of his existence had been set early in his life.

Jordan had been eight when his mother had died of pneumonia. His grandmother, herself in ill health, had contacted his father, Morgan Trent, in Chicago and informed him for the first time of the existence of his son.

To give the man credit, Morgan Trent immediately flew to the small Southern California town where Jordan had been born and lived. There had never been a question about Jordan's paternity. At eight, Jordan hadn't understood why this stranger had appeared one day, packed all of his belongings and taken him away from everything and everyone Jordan had known.

Morgan had explained that he was Jordan's father, but it hadn't really mattered to Jordan. He had gotten along without a father for eight years. Why did he need one now? Jordan could look back later from the vantage point of his thirty-five years and better appreciate what his father had tried to do for him.

Jordan hadn't been an easy child to get to know. An only child, he'd grown up learning how to keep himself busy without needing other people. His mother had worked long hours and he'd seen very little of her. His grandmother had been there to look after him, but she had never kept very close watch over where he went and how long he was gone.

So Jordan resented the sudden restrictions placed on him by his newly acquired father and stepmother. He didn't like their rules, their big home, and the fact that everything about their life was so formal.

He'd never seen the two of them share any affection or camaraderie. There was no spontaneity in the home, just stilted efforts at conversation.

Jordan willingly escaped by going away to school. He'd continued to be a loner there as well. His lifestyle had made him excellent recruiting material by the time he graduated from college.

With no close ties, he could easily disappear for weeks at a time without question. He deliberately chose women friends who were not inquisitive about his work and who showed no signs of possessiveness. He'd grown used to a certain type of woman with whom he was comfortable.

He knew nothing about a woman such as Lauren Mackenzie.

Jordan glanced at his watch. He needed to pick her up within the hour. They would catch the shuttle into New York, spend the night in the air and make connections for Vienna after they landed in Frankfurt.

He realized how strange he felt to be traveling so openly on commercial airlines. His previous excursions into Europe had been through military connections. There was something to be said for military travel, but not much.

Jordan checked the tickets Mallory had given him earlier. They were traveling first class. Interesting man. Jordan just wished he knew what Mallory was up to.

Lauren Mackenzie stood in front of her bathroom mirror and tried to come to terms with her new image. Her dark auburn hair had been lightened to a reddish blond. She had to get used to it immediately. It wouldn't help her believability if she kept doing a double take every time she caught sight of her image in a mirror.

The color wasn't the only thing that was different. Lauren had never given much thought to her hairstyle. She had thick, healthy hair that she'd always worn pulled away from her face. Now it was too short to be pulled back. Instead her hair feathered across her forehead and curled around her ears.

What a difference a haircut makes, she decided with a smile. Perhaps it paid to be cared for by professionals.

The woman who had shown her how to apply the makeup had complimented her on her glowing complexion. Since she shared the same skin tone as her mother and both her sisters, Lauren had always taken her complexion for granted. She knew that she could not tan. Instead she turned red, blistered and peeled. So while other women her age had been out by the pool or at the beach learning social repartee, Lauren had stayed inside, alone, and read.

Oh, well, Mr. Trent didn't seem to have a great abundance of social chitchat, either, if their meeting this afternoon had been any indication.

Drat! That was another thing. She couldn't keep referring to her husband as Mr. Trent. But she didn't like J.D., which was what Mallory called him. That put her in mind of a cigar-smoking wheeler-dealer—a kingpin-type, ruler of all he surveyed.

She'd seen his name on the passports they were given: Jordan Daniel Trent. She wondered if anyone called him Jordan? Daniel? Dan? Jordie? She shuddered at the thought of his reaction if anyone used that diminutive on him.

Glancing at her watch, Lauren hurriedly finished touching up her makeup and returned to her bedroom and the open suitcase on the bed. She couldn't get over the number of outfits they'd provided for her. The woman in charge of preparing her for the trip explained that everything had to look as though she and Jordan were typical American tourists, which meant they had money to afford a trip to Europe.

Lauren picked up the small pile of satin and lace that represented the colorful nightgowns she was expected to wear. Surely not in front of him? No one had said anything about their pretending to be married once they were alone in their hotel rooms. What if there was only one room?

She turned and hurriedly dug through one of her drawers. She'd take one of her own gowns just in case. Actually it was more of a nightshirt. Her sister had given it to her several years ago and it was faded, but the picture on it was still discernible. A familiar figure from the daily comics was sitting on her bed and speaking into a phone, saying, "I'm afraid I'm going to be late to work this morning. My hair won't start."

Meg had decided Lauren needed a little humor in her life. *Never more than right at this moment,* she thought, trying not to panic.

The doorbell rang and startled, she jumped several inches. *So much for nerves of steel,* she decided. Here she was doing the most adventurous thing in her life and she was determined not to be intimidated by the great unknown waiting for her out there. She'd never traveled overseas; in fact, her only vacations had been with her family.

What would her mom and dad think if they knew that she was going to be traveling with a man, pretending to be his wife? Who was she kidding? She knew exactly what they'd think. And who wouldn't?

She could just hear Meg and Amy now, teasing her about her extensive experience with men.

The doorbell rang again and Lauren rushed to the front door. Checking to make sure it was Mr. Trent—oops, uh, Jordan—she quickly unchained the door and opened it.

The clothes he was wearing were totally different from the casual attire he'd had on in the office earlier. The silvery gray suit emphasized his tanned skin and black eyes and hair. If he'd seemed imposing earlier, he looked downright intimidating now.

Lauren stepped back and motioned vaguely. "Come in," she said, pleased with the casual tone of her voice.

Jordan stepped inside so that Lauren could close the door, but he didn't take his eyes off her.

"What have they done to you?" he asked, his eyes narrowing slightly.

Now what? He didn't have to make his aversion to her quite so clear this early in their association. What did he think she would do, attack him at the first opportunity?

"Mr. Mallory told you that I would be made up to look like Frances Monroe."

"Does she dress like that?" he asked, a note of disbelief evident in his voice.

Lauren glanced down at the dress she had chosen to travel in. She'd been told it was wrinkle resistant, could be hand washed and dried quickly—all excellent attributes for a traveling outfit. Her chin came up. "What's wrong with the way I'm dressed?" she asked in an ominous tone.

Jordan realized, too late, that she was misjudging his reaction. The dark green dress did a creditable job of showing him that here was one woman who did not suffer from any figure flaws whatsoever. On the contrary. She would probably create a minor riot on a beach, if the curves shown to great advantage by the clinging dress were any indication of what lay underneath.

"Nothing. Not a thing. It just surprised me, that's all. I assumed that Mrs. Monroe was an older woman. That dress doesn't look . . . I mean—" Damn. He was getting himself in deeper with every utterance.

"Mrs. Monroe is in her mid-thirties, I believe."

"How old are you?"

"I don't see that my age has anything to do with this. I'm twenty-five."

"Oh. When I saw you earlier I thought you were—" Whoa. If you have any instincts for survival, you won't finish that statement, Trent, he thought.

"You thought I was—?" she repeated with unfeigned interest in her eyes.

"Uh, well, from what Mallory had told me, I just assumed that you were, uh, older."

"I see." She started toward the bedroom to get her suitcase, but paused in the doorway and looked back at him. "What difference does it make?"

"None," he assured her hastily. "None whatsoever!" Jordan watched her as she disappeared into the other room. Well, they were off to a flying start. He'd barely prevented himself from insulting her before they'd even left town.

Or at least he assumed she would feel insulted. How did a woman who looked like Lauren Mackenzie feel about herself? And what had been the purpose of that masquerade in the office? Come to think of it, he could see how her attractiveness might create a certain amount of distraction in the men who worked alongside her. Of course, it didn't affect him at all.

She reappeared in the doorway carrying her suitcase.

"Is that all you're taking?"

"I was told to travel as lightly as possible."

"Oh."

"Why?"

"I don't know. I just thought that women had to have a lot of luggage. At least the ones I've seen always travel with a half-dozen bags or so."

Lauren approached him and set the suitcase at his feet. "I think we should get something straight at the very beginning of our association, Mr. Trent. I do not appreciate being compared to all the other women in your life. By the same token, I will refrain from drawing any comparisons between you and the men that I happen to know."

Her cool tone and haughty manner incensed him. All he was trying to do was make small talk to break the ice. Instead the icicles rapidly forming from their conversation could almost be seen.

"Don't call me Mr. Trent, Lauren. I know all of this is new to you, but I'd appreciate your giving me a slim chance of pulling this charade off without your blowing our cover at the first opportunity."

She nodded. "Certainly. What shall I call you?"

He glanced at her in surprise. Didn't she even remember his name? He shrugged. "My friends call me Jordan."

"Aahhh. Your friends. I'm relieved to know you have some. Mr. Mallory gave me the impression you were the original lone wolf out in the wilds, working alone and preferring it that way."

"I am and I do. But contrary to what you may believe, I do happen to have acquired a few friends through the years."

Their voices had steadily become more clipped and cutting. Lauren gave him a brief flash of teeth in an effort to imitate a smile. "There's no accounting for taste, is there?" she said. "Shouldn't we be going?" she continued, glancing at her watch. "We don't want to miss our connections."

Jordan picked up her suitcase and headed toward the door. Lauren followed him, making sure the door was locked when they left the apartment.

At least I don't have to worry about accidentally endangering her on this trip, Jordan decided in the elevator. *I may end up murdering her myself before everything is over.*

By the time their plane left New York a few hours later, Lauren realized that she and Jordan had scarcely spoken to each other since leaving her apartment building.

This will never do, she thought ruefully. The flight attendants will probably think we've had a fight before we ever started this vacation.

She glanced at Jordan out of the corner of her eye. He had taken off his suit coat, loosened his tie, and seemed to be engrossed in a newspaper an attendant had handed to him. She stared unseeingly down at the magazine in her hands. Shouldn't they be talking, making plans, getting acquainted? Something?

Clearing her throat, Lauren said in a low voice, "Don't you think it would help if we shared some of our past history with each other? Just in case we're in a situation where it might be needed?"

Jordan slowly turned his gaze to her, his black eyes unreadable. She had a point—one he should already have thought of. Jordan couldn't understand his emotional reactions around this woman. His brain seemed to have taken a backseat to his feelings, which could get them both killed.

He nodded. "Why don't you start?" he suggested.

Feeling more than a little frustrated with his obvious reluctance to be the first to open up, Lauren began, "I was born and spent the first twenty-one years of my life in Pennsylvania. My parents still live in Reading. I have two sisters—I'm the one in the middle." She paused, trying to think of a way to summarize what was important in her life. "I'm very close to all my family. We try to get together as often as possible. My older sister is married; my younger one is in college."

"What are their names?" Jordan asked, surprised that he wanted to know more, that he was attempting to visualize her growing up.

Lauren raised her brows slightly. "Meg—Margaret—is the older one. She never answers to anything but Meg. And Amy is the youngest."

"Are they anything like you?"

"In looks? Disposition?" She shrugged slightly when he remained silent. "I suppose, a little in both. We seem to have inherited our dad's Scots temper along with the tinge of red in his hair."

"Are all of them mathematical geniuses?"

Lauren found herself studying his expression, trying to find any sarcasm in that question. She was surprised to see genuine interest. A movement behind his head caught her eye and she glanced up in time to see the smiling attendant pass by. Perhaps she had noticed their earlier silence and had decided they were now making up.

Perhaps they were.

"We all have an aptitude for figures. Meg put hers to use with her music. She plays several instruments quite well." She thought for a moment. "I don't know about Amy. She's the dreamy one, always floating around with her head in the clouds."

"Whereas you are logical and practical," he said with a slow smile that Lauren found rather endearing. It gave him a touch of vulnerability that she would not have guessed he harbored behind that stone-faced facade of his.

"I try, but sometimes my temper runs away with me." Impulsively she touched his arm that rested between them. "I'm sorry for my earlier remarks to you. I'm not usually that way with people I've just met. Somehow you managed to get under my skin."

His smile widened into a grin. "As long as we're talking about apologies, I owe you a couple myself. There was no reason to take out my frustration on you because of this assignment."

They sat there in silence for a few moments, studying each other.

"To tell you the truth," Lauren admitted after a while, "I did feel as though I'd been rather thrust upon you."

"For good reason. You were. I should be used to being overruled by now, though. Our working system certainly isn't set up as a democracy—the one man, one vote system. Whatever Mallory says goes."

"That didn't seem to stop you from trying to change his mind."

"That's because once in a while I've had success in convincing him that my plan is more workable."

Lauren shifted the magazine in her lap and the light caused a glint on her hand. Jordan reached over and took her left hand in his. A brilliant solitaire diamond sparkled on her ring finger, next to a gold band.

"Where did these come from?" he asked quietly.

Lauren grinned. "Why, darling, how could you have forgotten giving them to me on the most joyous occasion of my life!" She fluttered her lashes at him and gave him such a simpering smile that he began to laugh.

The change in him so astounded Lauren that she could only stare. Gone was the harsh-faced man she had met earlier in the day. Jordan's well-shaped mouth caught her attention, his white teeth a sharp contrast to his tanned face. His eyes sparkled and, for the first time, Lauren discovered how very attractive dark eyes could be. She was fascinated by this further glimpse of the man with whom she traveled.

"Now then," she said with a smile, "What about you? Any sisters? Brothers? Where did you grow up?"

The sudden cessation of all expression on his face stunned her. In less than a second he returned to being the cold, aloof man she'd met earlier.

As though reading from a prepared script, Jordan said, "I was born in California, moved to Chicago when I was eight, spent most of my growing-up years in boarding schools in New England."

"Oh." She hesitated for a moment, then asked, "Are your parents still alive?"

"My father is. My mom died when I was a child."

"Oh," she repeated, unsure of what to say. His voice betrayed no emotion. "So you're an only child?"

He nodded.

Lauren felt a chill surround her and she shivered slightly.

"Are you cold?" he asked, reaching overhead and turning the nozzle until there was no more air coming down on her.

"Thank you," she said softly.

"Would you like a pillow and blanket? We've got a long night ahead of us. I could use some sleep, myself. I seem to have spent the past forty-eight hours in the air." Jordan signaled the attendant who promptly provided them with the requested items.

"Jordan?" Lauren asked after they got settled in.

"Hmmm?"

"How long have we been married?" she asked softly.

He turned his head so that he was staring into her eyes, only a few inches away.

"I don't know. How long would you like to have been married?"

"Maybe three years? That would give us time to be used to each other, don't you think?"

"I have no idea. Three years is as good a time period as any, I suppose."

"Do we have any children?"

"No!" he answered abruptly.

"You don't want them?"

"Why are you asking all of these ridiculous questions, Lauren? How I feel about children is irrelevant to what we're doing!"

"Not necessarily. That would be something we would have talked about by now."

He sighed. "I'm beginning to see why you make a good cryptographer. You have to know all the answers, don't you?"

"Not all the time, no. But I do enjoy the challenge of working out a puzzle."

"Well, you can go to sleep now. Once we complete this little affair, I'll drop out of your life as quickly as I appeared. I'm not a puzzle that you have to figure out."

As Lauren pounded her pillow and built her nest against the bulkhead of the plane, she thought about Jordan's remarks. No doubt he was right. They weren't going to be together long enough for her to need to understand the type of person he was. However, Lauren had a strong hunch that she would be compelled to figure out what events in his life had made the man she saw today. The more she talked with him, the more protective layers she found wrapped around him.

Lauren closed her eyes and sighed. For some reason that she couldn't quite fathom, she wanted to get back in touch with the laughing man she'd caught a glimpse of earlier.

She knew that her insatiable curiosity had once again taken over and she wouldn't rest until she solved the intricate puzzle known as Jordan Trent.

Three

<hr />

They arrived in Frankfurt, Germany, in time for breakfast before catching their flight to Vienna.

Lauren didn't feel as though she'd slept at all. Somehow she must have. Otherwise she wouldn't have awakened in the morning light to find her head resting on Jordan's chest and his arms wrapped securely around her.

When had that happened?

As soon as she had shifted he'd immediately opened his eyes, fully alert. Lauren had never seen reflexes so finely tuned. She'd mumbled an apology for disturbing him and had gone to the restroom. The image she saw there dismayed her and she went to work to overcome the slept-in look she wore. After combing her hair and freshening her makeup, Lauren forced herself to return to her seat and the man waiting there for her.

Jordan excused himself without further comment and Lauren gave a quick sigh of relief. She needed the few minutes of privacy. Glancing at her watch, she knew they would be landing soon and the charade would begin in earnest. They would have to go through customs.

By the time they were seated and being waited on in the airport restaurant, Lauren had managed to calm down a little. The landing and going through customs hadn't been as bad as she had expected.

"How are you feeling?" Jordan asked, sipping his second cup of coffee.

"Much better than I was earlier. I don't know why I was so nervous. Customs wasn't so bad."

"Not this time, no. Every country has its own idiosyncrasies. And if we do go into Hungary or Czechoslovakia you'll find an entirely different attitude from the one we just encountered."

"Do you really think we'll go there?"

"I sincerely hope not, but I won't know until I've made a few contacts." He paused, looking around. "Which reminds me," he said in a lower voice. "From now on, even when you think we're alone, don't discuss what we're doing, okay?"

She nodded.

"Just remember that we're married and on vacation. Try to get into the part."

"I don't mind the vacation. The married part has me a little concerned."

His mouth twitched slightly. "Oh, really? You've managed to hide it well up until now."

"Yes, well, now that the time has come that I'm closer to sharing a room with you—"

"I know. But that can't be helped. Mallory was right. We need to stay as close to each other as possible. I'll have to leave you for short periods of time, but otherwise, we're going to be bosom buddies for the next few days."

Lauren noticed that his gaze idly dropped to her chest when he made his last remark and she could feel herself flushing. Damn him, anyway. Wasn't the situation awkward enough without his making innuendos?

"I should hope we'll at least have separate beds," she said, trying for a casual tone.

"Why? Do you pull covers?"

She just stared at him without replying.

His eyes narrowed slightly. "Don't tell me you've never shared a man's bed before."

Lauren could feel her face flushing with embarrassment.

Jordan lifted his hand to his forehead and groaned. "No, Mallory. No, you didn't do this to me!" He dropped his hand and glared at her. "Whatever possessed you to agree to be married to me when you've obviously had no experience?"

Lauren drew herself up and glared at him. "If I had been told I needed bedroom experience, believe me, I would never have consented to the plan. I was told they needed my help because of my resemblance to

Mrs. Monroe. There was never any discussion about how you and I would conduct ourselves!"

"I see," he said, amused at her indignation.

"If you need a woman, I'm sure you can find one elsewhere," she pointed out with prim dignity.

"Yes, that's true. Of course, I'm going to be fairly busy for the next few days so I probably won't be able to devote any of my time to the hunt." He made a barely perceptible shrug of feigned nonchalance. "However, I'll do my damnedest to contain my animal lusts." He could no longer conceal his smile. "Admittedly it will be tough for me since your luscious innocence will be around to tantalize me."

Jordan realized when he heard his words that he wasn't really jesting. Not that he had any intention of making love to her. Hell, he didn't even particularly like her, and despite some widely held beliefs of the general public regarding men in his occupation, he didn't go in for casual sex with anyone.

And he certainly did not intend to start something with a twenty-five year old virgin.

"I hope you're gaining some sort of amusement out of baiting me, Mr.—" He held up his hand suddenly and she amended her words. "—Jordan. I'm not in the least affected by your crude comments."

Her high color contradicted her lofty remarks, but he thought it best not to point that out. He was already in enough hot water. He didn't know why he enjoyed teasing her so much. Probably because she took the bait so easily.

Suddenly Jordan felt ashamed of himself. Here was a woman who was obviously out of her familiar mil-

ieu and handling herself very well. It must have taken
a great deal of courage for her to agree to come on this
trip with a complete stranger, a man who had made no
effort to make the situation any easier.

But he'd be damned if he would apologize! He
hadn't recruited her for this assignment. If she
couldn't say no, that was her problem.

A sudden vision of them in bed together flashed
before his mind. He had a hunch she would certainly
know how to say no if he tried anything at that time!

Noting that she was finished eating, he said, "Are
you ready?"

"Yes," she answered in a clipped voice.

Sighing, he stood and held out his hand. "My
mother never did manage to teach me many manners,
Lauren, but I am sorry if my teasing offended you."

Staring up at him, she slowly got to her feet and
placed her hand in his. She wrinkled her nose and
smiled. "I should be used to being teased by now. My
whole family is made up of notorious teases." Gently
withdrawing her hand, she said, "I just don't know
you well enough to know how to take what you say.
But I'll learn."

They were silent while he paid for their meal.
Walking down the concourse toward their gate, Jordan said, "You don't have to worry about my making
overtures toward you, Lauren. I would never take advantage of the situation."

She kept her head down for a moment, then glanced
up until she met his gaze. "Thank you, Jordan," she
said formally. "I appreciate your reassurance. And I
want you to have my reassurance," she went on in a

solemn voice, "that I will restrain my lusts as well so you will have nothing to worry about either."

Startled by her words, Jordan threw back his head and laughed, a full-throated, amused sound that caused more than one person to glance around at them. He threw his arm around her shoulders and hugged her to his side for a moment, then let go. Still laughing, he held out his hand for a handshake. "That's a real worry off my mind, Lauren, let me tell you. I'm relieved to know I'll be safe with you. Let's shake on it."

Once again Lauren had found the man she'd been shown a glimpse of earlier. She wondered how she could encourage that man to show up more often. She found him practically irresistible.

By the time they arrived at the hotel where they would be staying in Vienna, Lauren no longer cared who might end up sharing a bed with her. She cared only about finding a place to stretch out for a few hours. Her last full night's rest was a dim memory in her mind.

She knew she hadn't slept much since she'd been approached to make this trip. On more than one occasion she had suddenly decided to back out of the commitment. Only her strong sense of fair play and the idea that she would be able to help in a time of crisis had kept her going.

Now she was too tired to think about anything. She allowed Jordan to guide her in the right direction at the right time. Lauren was barely aware of anything by the time they reached the room.

"You're in luck, it seems. We won't have to fight over the covers tonight, anyway."

Lauren looked toward the beds that were side by side. She let her purse strap slide off her shoulder and as she watched the purse hit the floor she had no thought of trying to stop it.

Jordan walked over to her and lifted her chin so that he could look into her face. "You're exhausted, aren't you?"

Forcing her heavy eyelids open, Lauren noted with disgust that Jordan looked fresh and ready to go.

"Never mind. Why don't you stretch out for a while? I need to go out, anyway."

Lauren sank down on the side of the bed without saying a word.

"Don't you want to get into something more comfortable first?" he asked as she began to lower herself onto the pillow.

She closed her eyes with a sigh and groaned slightly.

He grinned and sat down beside her, slipping off her shoes. "Come on. I'll help you. You'll rest much better if—"

Lauren's eyes popped open and she slapped his hand away from her belt. "What do you think you're doing?"

"Helping my *wife*—" he emphasized the word, "—get more comfortable. Really, dear, you're certainly cranky when you're tired." There was a definite gleam in his black eyes.

Lauren was too exhausted to argue. Besides, he was right—about everything. Forcing herself into a sitting position, she began to unfasten her dress. Then she paused. "Am I expected to furnish your viewing entertainment while we're here?" she demanded to know.

He grinned and got to his feet. "Not at the moment, I'm afraid. I have to get going. I'll be late for my appointment."

"What—?" Lauren started to say when he suddenly leaned over and kissed her hard on the mouth. She was too startled to resist. By the time he pulled away from her, she could only stare at him in bemusement. Nuzzling her ear, he whispered, "You're going to have to go along with me, Lauren. Just trust that I know what I'm talking about. We can't afford to take any chances. Do you understand?"

She nodded and he straightened. "I'll see you later, darling," he said, then picked up the room key and left. She was still staring at the door when he opened it a few seconds later. "Don't go eat without me. I'll be back as soon as I can, okay?"

Lauren nodded her head like a puppet might, her movement jerky.

"Good girl," he said with a grin and closed the door once again. This time it stayed shut.

The kiss they had shared had shot a burst of adrenaline throughout her system and Lauren slid off the bed. She still felt as tired as ever, but decided to take a shower before going to sleep. By the time she returned to the bedroom she was pleasantly relaxed. Tucking her terry-cloth robe around her, she crawled under the covers and fell asleep, content to face whatever else the future had in store for her after some much needed rest.

A key turning in a lock awakened her sometime later and Lauren drowsily opened her eyes. For a moment she couldn't place where she was. In the deepening shadows of evening, the room seemed totally unfamiliar. Then the door opened and Jordan came in.

Lauren sat up in bed and switched on the lamp beside her.

"Hello," Jordan said. "Looks as though you managed to get some rest." He felt pleased that his tone sounded so casual. She looked so appealing sitting there, bathed in the soft light, her hair tousled and her eyes startled. He'd caught his breath at the first sight of her. Her gleaming skin seemed to call out to him, begging to be caressed. Except he knew better.

"I must have," she said, sounding confused. "What time is it?"

"Time for something to eat. How does that appeal to you?"

"Very much."

He opened his suitcase and sorted through it. "I'll take a quick shower, and then we'll see what we can find."

Lauren watched him disappear into the bathroom. After the door closed, she quickly left the bed and went to the closet where she had hung the clothes she'd brought with her. Dressing as though for a fire drill, Lauren was ready in moments. She took a little more time with her hair and makeup, but was still ready when he came out of the bathroom sometime later.

He'd chosen casual clothes that went along with the holiday spirit of their trip. The pull-over shirt fit his broad shoulders and chest very well. She hadn't been aware of his build until now.

Staying in good physical condition was no doubt part of his curriculum. Lauren just wished she wasn't so aware of him as a man. She was afraid her thoughts must be written on her face and she busied herself searching inside her purse.

"Have you misplaced something?" he asked, watching her.

"Oh, uh, no. I just wanted to make sure I had everything," she explained a little breathlessly.

"Ready?"

"Yes."

They were quiet until they reached the street. Jordan guided her to a car parked by the curb.

"Where did you get this?" she asked, surprised when he opened the door and motioned for her to get in.

"I wanted to feel a little less hampered in my movements, so I rented a car. Besides, we needed a place where we could talk."

As he drove through the streets of Vienna, Jordan explained, "You may think it silly, but I want us to assume that everywhere we go our conversation is being monitored, even in our room."

"Is that why—?"

"I kissed you this afternoon?" he ended for her. "Yes. We need to be aware of where we are and what we're attempting to do."

"Were you able to get any information this afternoon about Mrs. Monroe?"

"Some, which is another reason for the car. We're going to Brno in the morning."

"Where's that?"

"In Czechoslovakia."

"Is that where she is?"

"There's a strong possibility. Enough to check out the lead."

"Then your friends were able to help."

"Hardly friends, innocent. Some people would sell their mother if the price was right."

"Oh."

"Sorry if I disillusioned you about human nature," he said after several minutes of silence.

"It isn't that, exactly. I was just thinking how much I take my family and my life-style for granted. Nothing very exciting has ever really happened in our lives. We've just gone through life accepting our homes and jobs and friends without question. I've never really thought about how other people live."

"You'll find the same types all over the world, Lauren. In my profession, I happen to deal with a different type of human being than you've ever had occasion to meet." He muttered something under his breath and she looked around at him, noting his grim profile.

"What did you say?"

"I just said I hope you don't have to meet them. But under the circumstances I don't see how I can protect you from the possibility."

She smiled. "I'm a grown woman, you know. I don't need protecting."

"Hang on to that thought, honey. You're probably going to need it."

The restaurant they chose was quiet. They were early for the dinner hour, which was fine with Lauren. It gave her a chance to get used to being in a new place without feeling that everyone knew she was a foreigner.

"Have you been in touch with Mr. Mallory?" she asked over dessert.

"Indirectly."

"Have they received any more news regarding the lady in question?"

"No."

"Oh. Then no one has any idea who might be responsible," she said in a low voice.

"I don't want to start naming names at the moment, but I have some strong ideas. Let's just say the sooner we find her, the better off she'll be."

Lauren shuddered at his grim tone and the look on his face. Here was one man she would definitely not want as an enemy.

How about as a lover? a small voice seemed to whisper inside her head. The thought shocked her. Lauren didn't think of men in that context. The few with whom she had made friends were casual acquaintances, usually with romantic ties to someone else.

When it came right down to it, she really didn't know much about men, she decided. Fathers don't count. She smiled at the thought.

"I would love to know what's going on in that pretty head of yours," Jordan said softly, watching the changing expressions on her candlelit face.

When the color rose to her cheeks, he grinned. "I bet they're worth a great deal more than a penny."

"I doubt that," she said, trying not to stammer. "Actually I was thinking about my parents," she said, only stretching the truth slightly. "I'm going to find it very difficult not telling them about my visit to Europe once I get home."

"It would be a little difficult to explain, wouldn't it?"

"Yes. Mr. Mallory told me to tell everyone I was going to California for some additional training."

"Makes sense, I suppose. One of his most adhered to policies is the 'need-to-know' one. Less chance of a slipup somewhere."

"Yes, he explained that to me. I understand the reasons," she said, glancing around the luxurious restaurant ruefully.

"Well, maybe you can come back some other time," he suggested.

"Somehow I doubt it."

"Insist on spending your honeymoon in Vienna," he said facetiously.

She stared at the way the candlelight was reflected in his eyes and suddenly realized that despite the less than auspicious start of their relationship, she would never think of Vienna without remembering Jordan Trent.

Glancing down at the expensive tablecloth in front of her, she absently reached for her coffee.

"Lauren?"

His low tone made her look up at him, startled.

"I'm sorry. Did I touch a sore point with you? I seem to have a real knack for offending you without knowing exactly how."

"You didn't offend me."

"But something about a honeymoon in Europe did."

She shook her head. "No, not really. I was just thinking how remote the possibility would be, that's all."

"Why?"

She shrugged. "I'm just one of those people who will stay single all her life."

He muttered a word that was unprintable but succinct. She met his gaze in surprise at his quietly spoken vehemence.

"I take it some idiot broke your heart and you're determined never to trust another man."

Her sudden peal of laughter startled him. It was the first time he'd seen her genuinely amused. He found her adorable. Baffling, but adorable.

"You couldn't be more wrong," she finally managed to say.

"Oh?"

"Look at me. I'm not the type of woman men go for, surely you recognize that."

Jordan had a sudden image of Lauren the first time he saw her—glasses, boxy suit, low-heeled shoes, careless hairdo and he almost flinched at his remembered reaction to her. How could he have missed the beauty of her eyes that reminded him of the soft mist of early dawn, or the velvety softness of her cheek that caused his hand to itch from wanting to touch it. And that figure. Were all men blind? Then he remembered her deliberate camouflage.

Lauren Mackenzie was like a hidden treasure that had suddenly been exposed to light. She glittered and gleamed with newness, wholesomeness, vitality. Would he ever forget her sense of humor?

"It depends on the man," he said slowly, carefully thinking through what he wanted to say. "A man of discernment would recognize what a prize you are, Lauren. You have a great deal to offer the man lucky enough to win your love."

He sounded very sincere, yet the words seemed so peculiar coming from him. They reminded her of some of the heart-to-heart talks she'd had with her father.

That was it. He was trying to be reassuring and kind, which rather surprised her. Kindness certainly hadn't seemed to be one of his character traits.

She smiled. "I'm not sure what to say. You've quite taken my breath away with your lovely words." Her tone was teasing but her eyes reflected her vulnerability.

No longer able to resist the temptation, Jordan reached across the small table and brushed his knuckles against her cheek. He'd been right. Her skin felt like velvet. He could feel himself reacting to the touch and he hastily lowered his hand.

"Are you ready to go?" he asked briskly, glancing around the room.

The sudden mood transition caused a small ache to appear somewhere in the region of Lauren's heart. What had she expected, anyway? He was still doing his best to pretend a husbandly affection. She needed to remember that their time together was a charade and temporary. Sort of a momentary marriage that would end as soon as their mission was completed.

Four

—

Lauren noticed that Jordan had very little to say on the return trip to their hotel. Of course he could be tired, since he hadn't had the benefit of the nap she had enjoyed.

When they arrived, he escorted her in silence through the lobby, into the elevator and down the hallway to their room. Only when they reached their door did she sense a change in him.

"What is it?" she said, almost whispering in the quietness of the hallway.

Without saying a word he motioned for her to stand to the side of him. He inserted the key and turned the knob, shoving the door open without entering.

When nothing happened, he flicked on the light and glanced around the room, then relaxed.

"What is it?" she repeated, ashamed to hear the slight tremble in her voice.

He shook his head and chuckled. "Paranoia setting in." He waved to their beds, which had been turned down for them. "Obviously the maid has been here since we left."

"How did you know someone had been in the room?" she asked, looking around uncertainly.

"I knew," he said in a flat tone of voice. "Look, I'm going to have to leave you again. There was someone waiting downstairs I need to see."

She didn't know whether that was true or not, but it didn't matter.

"You'll be all right alone?" he asked.

"Of course."

He nodded, walked into the bathroom and looked around, returned to the bedroom, checked under the beds and inside the closet. "I'll see you later."

Lauren began to prepare for bed in a thoughtful mood. Deciding to relax in a steaming bath, she carried her nightclothes into the bathroom with her and closed the door.

She had just seen another side of Jordan's personality, one that frightened her with its intensity. The professional had peered out at her and she began to have some inkling why Mr. Mallory had insisted on sending him to Europe.

By the time Lauren completed her bath, she was pleasantly drowsy. Pleased that she had bought a book at the airport in New York, she began to read, unaware that she was listening for his footstep outside the door.

Eventually her fatigue overcame her and she closed the book, turned off the light and wiggled down under the covers. If this was an example of marriage, Lauren decided sleepily, she would do just as well to continue to live alone.

Lauren woke up sometime during the night and realized that Jordan had returned while she slept. She saw his reassuring bulk in the bed beside her. He was so close she could have reached out and touched his back as he lay turned away from her.

How amazing! She felt protected immediately, knowing he was nearby. Shifting to find a more comfortable position, she drifted off to sleep once again.

Jordan knew that Lauren had awakened, but he didn't move. He'd awakened instantly at the subtle change in her breathing. It was a habit he couldn't seem to break, nor did he want to. His skill at being aware of someone else in a room had come into play more than once in his career. It was second nature to him now.

Lauren hadn't stirred when he'd come in earlier. He'd undressed in the bathroom, realizing that he'd have to sleep in his briefs. He was certain that Lauren wouldn't appreciate waking up to his nude body come morning.

The man he'd seen loitering outside the hotel when they'd returned had given him some valuable information—if it could be believed. Jordan felt the man was more trustworthy than some he'd dealt with in the past. The man felt that Jordan had once saved his life.

Jordan's memory was a little hazy about the matter but he was willing to accept the man's help, whatever his reasons.

Now, at least, he had been given a possible address where Mrs. Monroe might be. Jordan didn't want to think about her state of mind or physical condition. There was nothing he could do about that. He would find her, then make any necessary decisions.

He caught the sound of Lauren's regular breathing once more and he relaxed. Turning onto his back he lay there, staring up at the darkened ceiling. This was a new experience for him, lying next to a warm, desirable woman and not touching her.

Jordan found it disconcerting how much he did want to touch her. The quick kiss they had shared that afternoon had unnerved him more than he had wanted to admit at the time. Her lips had been so soft and giving. It had taken a great deal of willpower to end the kiss and pull away from her. He'd already made a promise to her and he intended to keep it.

He just wished he didn't find her quite so attractive.

The sound of a shattering explosion that seemed to be right there in their room caused immediate reactions in both Lauren and Jordan. Lauren screamed. Jordan was on his feet, pistol in hand, checking the room and eventually looking out their window down at the street.

Lauren threw herself out of the bed and ran to where he stood. "What was that?" she cried, trembling violently.

Absently placing his free arm around her shoulders, he pulled her close to his almost-bare body. "An explosion of some kind," he muttered in an absent tone, continuing to watch as people began to gather from all directions. He tried to make out what the shouts were but the sounds weren't clear enough.

Lauren suddenly realized she was pressed tightly to a well-built, unadorned male. Her thigh-length nightshirt prevented most of her from touching him directly, but she could feel the hair on his thigh brushing against her.

"Well," she said shakily, trying to move away from his firm grip without success, "I didn't think it was your travel alarm." Now that she realized she hadn't been a part of the explosion, Lauren tried to calm down, but her heart wasn't having any part of the calming exercise. Not as long as she was so intimately clutched to the tall male holding her. Then her eyes focused on his other hand.

"Where did you get that?" she asked, nodding toward the pistol.

"I brought it with me," he said, still watching the street.

"Isn't that illegal?"

"Not necessarily."

"You didn't declare it."

"No."

"Then it was illegal."

"Only if you get caught."

"An interesting use of logic," she managed to say. When he didn't seem to have any intention of letting her go, she asked, a little breathless from trying to talk calmly when she felt anything but calm, "Would you kindly let me go?"

He looked down at her in surprise as though amazed to find her tucked so closely next to him. He also realized that neither of them had many clothes on. Jordan stepped away from her as though she had suddenly scorched his fingers.

"Hey, lady," he spread his hand out as if to reassure her, "you're the one who ran to me, remember?"

"I know. I wasn't accusing you of anything." She paused. "I really was afraid."

"So was I," he said, walking over to his side of the bed and picking up the pair of pants he'd left there. Placing the gun on the table, he stepped into the pants, zipped them, then turned around and faced her.

"I didn't think people like you were ever afraid of anything," she said.

"People like me," he repeated in a steady voice, "are just as human as the rest of you. We have thoughts and feelings. We feel pain when we get hurt, bleed like any mortal being."

They stood looking at each other and Lauren didn't know what to say. Whether it was because of the unorthodox way they'd been awakened, or the early hour, she didn't know. But something had changed between them. There was a tension that hadn't been there before. She didn't understand it—where it came from, or why it was there—but she could sense its presence as though another person had entered the room and joined them.

Lauren padded quietly over to him and placed her hands on his bare chest. "I didn't mean to imply that I think of you as something less than human."

"Didn't you?"

She shook her head. His face was hard and without expression, but somewhere in his eyes a small flash of pain—of vulnerability—seemed to appear momentarily, then was gone. She would never have seen it if she hadn't been so close to him.

Never before had Lauren felt such a need to comfort someone. She forgot that this man was fiercely independent, a loner who fought his own battles and invariably won. What she had seen was a glimpse of the small boy who had learned a harsh lesson at a very early age: life didn't always guarantee a happy ending.

Going up on tiptoe, Lauren placed her lips softly against his, wanting him to know that she cared, that she was in no way judging him or his life-style. She slipped her hands up so that they encircled his neck.

Totally bemused by her uncharacteristic actions, Jordan was at a loss as to how to respond to her. What in the hell did she think she was doing, anyway? Did she believe a kiss would make everything all right—like a child who thinks that mommy can kiss it and make it better?

Whatever her motives, he could not remain unaffected by her closeness. His arms closed around her and he responded to her with an urgency that surprised them both. He took over the kiss, showing her how, teaching her to open her mouth for him.

He felt, more than heard, the soft gasp she gave but he was too much involved with the scent and taste of her to acknowledge her surprise. She felt wonderful in his arms.

His hands roamed restlessly up and down her spine as his mouth explored hers. When he was forced to draw away for breath, he continued to kiss her cheeks, her eyes, the soft hollow of her neck, then he returned his mouth to hers, having missed its soft sweetness. He felt the tiny quivering of her lower lip as he took possession once more.

Without conscious thought of the implications of what he was doing, Jordan swept Lauren up and placed her on his bed, following her down without ever losing contact with her.

Lauren had never before felt such a swirl of emotions. She'd had no idea a kiss could cause such a violent reaction within her body. Her legs were trembling so that her knees had almost given way by the time he lifted her in his arms.

She'd had no idea that a man's hands could evoke so many sensations. His touch set off tiny electrical sparks beneath her skin as though small units of energy were being snapped on after lying dormant for the past twenty-five years. Her body seemed to understand what was happening and was responding to him.

Lauren lightly traced the musculature of his back and shoulders, intrigued with the interplay of smooth skin and taut muscles beneath her fingers. They found the slight indentation of his spine that created an alluring path for her fingers to follow down his back until they reached the waistline of his trousers. Undeterred, she followed a path around to his stomach. His involuntary movement, flinching at her touch, caused her to pause.

"Don't stop," he managed to mutter in her ear. "I'm just very, very sensitive in that area." He followed his words with like action, running his hand along her thigh and under her short gown until he found the sensitive skin around her navel.

Oh, yes! Now she understood just how sensitive skin could be to a touch. And such a light touch, as well. How strange. And how wonderful.

Growing bolder she explored his chest, enjoying the feel of the mat of hair that covered it, as black and as curly as the hair on his head. He was such a wonderful example of virile manhood. Lauren had never known anyone even remotely like him.

When he tugged on her gown she immediately raised her arms so that he could pull the garment over her head. Tossing the gown on the floor and removing the pants he'd put on earlier, Jordan turned back to her, pulling her closer to him. Her eyes were closed, her expression dreamy. They lay on the rumpled sheets, his thigh between hers, his arm beneath her shoulders. All he could do was to drink in the sight of her ivory-colored skin, highlighted by the dim glow of the early morning dawn from the window.

Gently he touched the rose-colored tip of her breast with his finger and watched as she caught her breath. God, she was lovely, so lovely, so desirable. And he wanted her very, very much.

Jordan leaned over and with his tongue lightly traced a circle around the rosy tip. Lauren gave a soft sigh and placed her hands in his hair, holding him close to her. Encouraged, he continued to explore, enjoying the moment, helpless to prevent what was happening between them.

Time lost all meaning as they learned how to please each other. There was no doubt in Jordan's mind that Lauren was totally untutored. Nor was there any doubt but that she was quite willing for him to show her what she had been unaware of all these years.

Jordan didn't question why a woman who had held herself aloof from other men would be willing to give herself to him. At the moment it was enough that they were together.

He was in no hurry to consummate their lovemaking. He wanted her to enjoy it and he refused to rush, which was why they were both still wearing their briefs when there was a sudden pounding on the door.

They sprang apart as though a sudden shower of ice water had hit them.

"Who is it?" Jordan roared, ready to kill whoever it was that had interrupted them at that moment.

In heavily accented English a man said, "I am from the police and wish to speak with you, Mr. Trent."

They gazed at each other, Lauren with horrified dismay, and Jordan with a great deal of disgust. Whatever the police wanted, it was certain to delay their plans for leaving the country later that morning.

"Just a moment, please," he said, getting up and pulling on his pants. As he walked by her bed, he reached down and picked up the terry cloth robe that had fallen off during the night. "Let's don't give them any more than their hearts can stand this early in the morning, honey."

Glancing around the room, he saw his pistol still lying on the table beside his bed. In a few swift movements he grabbed it and, reaching into his suitcase, moved something in the bottom of the case and placed the gun there.

Lauren had never experienced such a confusion of emotions in her life. She pulled on the robe and hastily tied the sash, then watched the door apprehensively as Jordan walked over to it.

After offering identification, two plainclothesmen stepped inside the room.

"I'm sorry to awaken you so early, Mr. Trent," the spokesman began. "However, we didn't think it possible that anyone could have slept through the explosion."

"We weren't asleep, exactly," Jordan said, glancing over at his bed, which showed definite signs of double occupancy. Lauren could not remember ever having been so embarrassed in her life.

"Ah, yes, of course," the policeman said with a polite smile. "We are quite sorry to interrupt you and your wife."

"What seems to be the problem?" Jordan asked, motioning to the small grouping of chairs and sinking down on the side of Lauren's bed. She continued to stand by the side of his bed, restlessly twisting the sash of her robe.

"I'm afraid that the explosion caused some damage to the car you rented yesterday."

"I see. What was the explosion? Do you know?"

"It is under investigation, of course. A car bomb. Luckily no one was killed. However, there was considerable damage to nearby cars and buildings."

"Do you have incidents like this often?"

The man shrugged. "What is often? Once is too often as far as I'm concerned."

"Of course you're right. We're from Chicago and can certainly understand some of the problems the police have to deal with."

The man nodded. "If you would like, we could see what can be done about getting you another car. Were you planning to spend a few days here in Vienna before continuing your travels?"

The seemingly innocent question set off an alarm in Jordan's head. There was nothing to prevent a local policeman from working with others whose political beliefs were different from those held in his own country.

Jordan forced himself to smile and say, "Yes, we're hoping to stay about a week. Of course we do intend to explore the countryside, see some of the beautiful sights that Austria has to offer."

"Good. That is very good. We are just so sorry that your first night here must be so violent."

Jordan shrugged. "Let's hope the rest of our stay is more peaceful."

The two policemen stood and walked to the door. Jordan followed them.

Once again, the spokesman said, "Please accept our apologies—for the damage to the car and for our untimely intrusion." His eyes flickered to Lauren without expression, then back to Jordan.

Jordan opened the door for them, exchanging the usual pleasantries about the remainder of their visit. When he finally closed and locked the door, he heard Lauren move behind him.

Without saying a word he took her hand and led her into the bathroom. Reaching into the tub he turned on the water, then turned back to her and drew her close to him.

"There's a better than usual chance that this room has surveillance equipment in it. I don't know if we're being watched because of the timing of our arrival and the bombing, but it's obvious we've been checked out by the local authorities. Someone may suspect why we're here." He silently added that if the latter were the case, Jordan and Lauren didn't have a hope in hell of succeeding with their plan.

"What do we do now?" she whispered, her face without color.

Jordan wished he could suggest that they continue where they'd left off—but he knew better—for several reasons. One, the mood was gone—their possible danger now occupied their thoughts. Two, Jordan wasn't at all sure that he could handle having a relationship, however temporary, with Lauren Mackenzie. He'd never reacted to a woman before the way he did to her.

Of course he found her physically attractive, but there was so much more than that as he'd discovered this morning. He felt so protective of her. He admired her, not only for her beauty, but for her intelligence, her wit and her ability to immediately grasp a situation.

She was nothing like the women he was ordinarily involved with. And more importantly, he knew that he was the first man she'd been with.

Whatever possessed her to come to him so willingly? What did she expect from him? Whatever it was, he couldn't give it to her. Their lives were poles apart. They had nothing in common. And once they got through the next few days, they would never see each other again.

It was up to him to maintain some sort of control while they were together. That was going to add another burden to an already tough assignment.

He reached over and turned off the water. "How does breakfast sound?" he asked in a cheerful voice that sounded loud in the small bathroom.

She tried to respond to his light note with a smile, but it was hard won. "Sounds good," she said.

He leaned over and kissed the tip of her nose. "Good girl," he whispered, then straightened. "If you'll excuse me, I'll get shaved so we can go downstairs."

She nodded, still obedient to his remarks, and left the room.

When Jordan closed the door he leaned against it and sighed.

He wished he understood what was happening to him. No woman had ever affected him like this before. He didn't like it. He didn't like it at all.

Five

Lauren entered the bedroom, feeling dazed. So many things had happened in such a short period of time.

Her serene, orderly existence had exploded much like the bomb that had gone off earlier that morning. Lauren sank down on the edge of the bed and stared unseeingly at the wall.

Until now her life had been governed by her logical thinking processes. What had happened to her?

Lauren Mackenzie had grown up being treated as someone different from her peers by her teachers and classmates. What came easy for her, others found difficult to do. By the time she had finished high school Lauren had accepted that although the males she knew might be friendly to her, especially when they needed help with their homework, she wasn't the type of woman men found attractive.

Of course her parents had tried to reassure her on this point, but Lauren's logical mind continued to collect evidence to support her theory all during college. By the time she had accepted the offer made by the agency a few years ago, Lauren had resigned herself to her permanently single state and had dismissed the matter from her mind. Since there was nothing she could do about being who she was, she forgot about it. She dressed for comfort, not style, and she made friends with people who interested her, rather than with those who could advance her career.

Lauren had been surprised when Mr. Mallory approached her and asked for her help. She'd been even more surprised when he'd explained what he wanted her to do. He wanted her to pretend to be somebody's wife?

How laughable! Lauren had never even been on a date. When Mr. Mallory began to describe Jordan Trent to her, the unreality of the situation intensified. She wouldn't have been at all surprised to find a giant S on Jordan's undershirt. Mallory had convinced her that Jordan was the best operative they had and that he could be counted on to successfully conclude the assignment.

The next shock was meeting Jordan Trent and facing his anger over her role in the assignment. She'd never been exposed to a man of his nature who made his living in such a manner. She'd been in awe of him until he'd provoked her anger.

What she hadn't expected to find was his sense of humor. Even more of a shock to her was the vulnerability she had glimpsed in him.

As soon as she'd seen the sensitivity he kept so carefully hidden from the world she was able to relate to him. Both of them had learned to function well in their own fields, without allowing those around them ever to get to know the real person hiding his and her thoughts and feelings from the world.

Lauren had instinctively reached out to that person in Jordan that morning in an attempt to let him know that she understood. His physical response and her shattering reaction to him had created more of a shock to her system than the bomb exploding or the police pounding on their door.

He'd been physically attracted to her, of that she had no doubt. He'd been tender and gentle and yet his touch had forcibly shown Lauren an undeveloped side of her nature. She had never felt that way before. How extraordinary and totally out of character.

She felt as though she'd been at a masquerade party and, when Jordan admitted to being afraid, he had removed his mask for her. For the first time she recognized that they were more alike than she could possibly have imagined. She had found her other half.

So this is what it feels like, she thought, glancing down at the pillow she and Jordan had shared such a short time ago.

She suddenly remembered a scene from her childhood. She'd been sitting watching her mother prepare several varieties of cookies for the school bake sale. And the young Lauren had asked, "How long did you know Dad before you knew you were in love with him?"

Hilary Mackenzie had smiled the smile that always meant she was thinking of her husband. "Not nearly as long as it took him to recognize what he was feeling," she replied.

"How did the two of you meet?"

"Your father was working with a group of men who went from farm to farm helping with the hay harvest. They arrived one day to go to work on my father's farm."

The young Lauren sighed. "And it was love at first sight, I bet."

"Hardly. I thought he was the most obnoxious man I'd ever met. I'd just turned sixteen, you understand, and was extremely aware of my own dignity, which your father insisted on poking fun at."

"That sounds like Daddy, all right."

"Yes. He's always been a terrible tease. I felt he must have decided he had a special calling to make my life miserable, because he certainly made a career of it that summer." Hilary shook her head, remembering.

"So when did you change?"

Her mother was quiet for a moment, gazing out the window, not seeing anything but her memories. "Even now I can remember the exact moment when I knew that I loved Matt Mackenzie. The sun was setting and the men were walking in from the fields, all hot and dirty. The other men were ahead of him so that when I saw him he was alone, walking that winding path up toward the house, the sun behind him. He was little more than a silhouette." Her mother glanced down at the bowl of dough before her as though wondering where it had come from.

"I knew it was him by the way he walked," she continued. "The way he held his head, so proud and arrogant like, so full of himself as I always tell him. The sun seemed to make his hair shine even brighter red than usual, almost like a halo."

Hilary looked over at her daughter with a sheepish expression on her face. "I can't explain it, even now, but somehow, seeing him coming toward me I just knew that I loved him. That I'd always love him, no matter what."

"Then what happened?" Lauren had asked eagerly.

"Nothing."

"Oh, Mama, don't say that. Of course something happened. You married him, didn't you?"

Hilary smiled. "Not that summer, I didn't; you can be sure of that."

"Did you tell him how you felt?"

"I didn't have to. I guess he saw the change in me. Where once I got angry at his teasing, after that I'd just laugh. I started talking with him more, rather than avoiding him. I began to ask questions about him because I was interested."

"And then?"

"And then summer was over and he was gone— back to college in Pennsylvania."

"So how did the two of you ever get together?"

"He started writing to me and I answered him. Then, during spring break, he came out to Nebraska to see me and I knew that I was more than just a friend to him, but I didn't really know how he felt."

"Did he tell you?"

"Are you kidding? Matt would never be serious long enough to tell me how he really felt. I guess men sometimes have trouble finding the words to express how they feel."

"So when did he propose?"

"He didn't."

"Mother!" Lauren could well recall her shock.

"He started writing letters with little phrases like 'after we're married—' or 'we'll have to name our firstborn Margaret Ann after my maternal grandmother' or 'I hope you won't mind living in Pennsylvania. It looks like I've found a pretty good job here as soon as I graduate.'"

Lauren began to laugh. "That sounds just like him."

Hilary nodded. "Yes. When he wrote and asked me if I had any objections to getting married in June after he graduated, I told him no, I had no objections at all."

"Did he ever tell you he loved you?"

Hilary smiled that special smile. "He never had to tell me, sweetheart. He showed it in every way that counts."

"He really does show it, doesn't he, Mama?"

Hilary nodded. "He really does."

Staring at a pillow on a rumpled bed in Vienna, Austria, Lauren recalled that conversation with her mother as though she'd just had it.

How do you know when you're in love?

She had known without a doubt. When she saw that flash of vulnerability in Jordan's eyes, every irritating thought she'd ever had about him had seemed to disappear. She knew that she loved him, would always love him and without consciously deciding, she had offered herself to him free of reservation.

What must he have thought of her? she wondered, turning to the closet and reaching for something to wear. After all of her silly remarks about sharing a room with him, the first time she had the opportunity she threw herself at him.

She knew that he wasn't the type of man who would turn down such an offer. He couldn't fake his obvious response to her. Even in her innocence she recognized that.

The question was, what was she going to do now? She certainly couldn't expect Jordan to fall in love with her just because she wanted things to work out that way. Lauren was too much of a realist to even consider the possibility.

They had nothing in common. Even though Lauren had never really expected to marry, there had been times when she had yearned for a child or two to care for—who would share with her the abundant love she had.

Jordan had made it clear how he felt about children. His life-style wasn't conducive to a quiet home life filled with the laughter of children and the chores associated with a home. Somehow she couldn't picture Jordan mowing a lawn or trimming a hedge or tinkering with a bicycle.

Lauren should feel relieved that the interruption had come when it did. But instead she felt robbed. She forced herself to face the fact that if she could have nothing more than these few days with Jordan Trent, she wanted them with a ferocity that surprised her.

Logically and rationally her decision made no sense whatsoever. But then love could never be explained away, either logically or rationally.

She heard the door to the bathroom open and caught a whiff of Jordan's aftershave. She would never smell that well-known brand again that she wouldn't be reminded of him.

He walked out and stopped just inside the bedroom. She still wore her robe. "Sorry I took so long," he said, rubbing his jaw slowly.

She forced herself to smile lightly. "No problem. I'll hurry," she said, matching her steps to her words as she went by him.

He stopped her by placing his hand lightly on her arm. "Lauren?"

She met his eyes squarely. "Yes?"

"About what happened earlier..."

"Yes?"

Damn, he wished she wouldn't look at him with that clear-eyed gaze that seemed to look deep inside of him. "I'm sorry. I didn't mean to take advantage of—"

"You didn't," she said quickly, interrupting him. "If you'll recall, I'm the one who started it. I guess you'll have trouble trusting me again, huh?" she asked.

She wasn't angry! He couldn't believe it. In fact, she was teasing him. Here he'd spent all this time wrestling with his conscience, determined to make the right decision for everyone concerned, and she was treating the whole thing as though it didn't matter.

"Something like that," he said slowly, watching her closely.

"I'm sorry if it embarrassed you," she said quietly.

"Embarrassed me! Of course not. It's just that this situation is a little unusual. We have to think about—" He stopped himself and glanced around, suddenly remembering that he had to be careful what he said. He shrugged. "Go ahead. We can talk later."

She walked into the bathroom and turned to shut the door. "There's really nothing to talk about, is there? Nothing really happened."

Jordan watched the door close before turning to his suitcase. *Oh, yeah, Miss Innocence? That's what you think,* he grumbled to himself.

Before, he'd only had his imagination to fuel the flames she seemed to ignite inside him. Now he knew exactly what was underneath those attractive dresses she wore.

What he couldn't understand was what a woman like Lauren Mackenzie was doing unattached. If he were the settling down kind, she'd be the first— But that way of thinking was a waste of energy. He wasn't the settling down type. And she deserved better than he could offer.

Jordan found a shirt and socks and put on his shoes, then waited for her to reappear.

It was almost like being married.

When they entered the lobby there were people milling around, all talking excitedly. A cordon of uniformed policemen watched as a crew cleared the debris of glass and other building materials from around the entrance to the hotel.

Jordan guided Lauren into the dining area of the hotel where they were served breakfast.

After the waiter left, Lauren asked, "What do we do now?"

Jordan enjoyed his first sip of coffee before answering her. "I need to get another car and then you, my dear, will start earning your keep on this trip."

Her eyes widened slightly, unsure of his meaning. Whether he was teasing her or not she was ready to do whatever she could.

"All right," she said with a nod.

He grinned. "Shouldn't you ask what it is first?"

"I don't have to," she replied calmly.

Her calm acceptance, which showed a great deal of trust in him, almost unnerved him.

"I haven't had any trouble so far since I speak German," he began, "and I know a smattering of many of the languages in Europe. But to get detailed information, I'll need your help once we get into Czechoslovakia."

She smiled. "All right."

"Do you know the Slavic languages spoken there?"

"I've studied them, yes. I haven't had much practice in recent years, but I'm sure they will come back."

"Fine."

Within the hour they were on their way north to Brno, Czechoslovakia.

Jordan had kept their room in Vienna, and casually dropped the information that they would be exploring the countryside and might end up staying at some village inn somewhere. They repacked so that they could share Jordan's suitcase. Lauren had been shaken by the intimacy of their apparel resting so cozily together and had to remind herself that appearances meant a great deal in a situation such as theirs.

Lauren discovered that she enjoyed the drive through the peaceful countryside. Jordan shared with her some of the experiences he had had while working in Europe. He also gave her tips on what to expect behind the iron curtain, how to behave, and instructions in case of an unexpected crisis.

"I know someone to contact in Brno, which helps. He seems able to keep his finger on the pulse of the city. Nothing happens that he doesn't know about. If Frances Monroe was taken there, he'll know."

The closer they drew to the border, the quieter they became. There was only so much rehearsing they could do. Now was the time to start acting for all they were worth.

Lauren discovered that she was comfortable pretending to be Jordan's wife. She loved him and she could pretend for the next little while that the relationship was real.

Jordan wished he were going in alone. There were too many unknowns in the situation.

Mallory had been wise to suggest they stay with their real names and backgrounds. Jordan had posed as a sales representative from Chicago, Illinois for so many years that he found it easy to fall back into that role.

Now he and his wife were in Europe on vacation. He intended to mention that they had some friends in Chicago who had relatives living in Brno, in case anyone asked. Otherwise, they were just visiting a town known for its manufacturing business. What better place for a sales rep to want to visit?

Crossing the border took a little time. Their car and suitcase were minutely inspected. Passports were scrutinized and the papers on the car were carefully read. Eventually they were allowed to go on their way.

"I think it helped that you knew their language," Jordan remarked as they drove away. "Claiming that you had a grandmother born in Pizen helped."

"It was true," she said quietly.

He glanced around in surprise. "Why hadn't you told me before?"

"It never occurred to me," she admitted.

"And what other fascinating background have you yet to reveal to your husband?" he asked with a grin.

"Nothing of any interest, I'm sure."

Jordan thought about that as they continued their journey. She was wrong. He found everything about her interesting. Lauren was such an unusual blend of innocence and sophistication, intelligence and naïveté, that he never knew what to expect from her next.

His traitorous mind reverted to the early morning hours and once again Jordan experienced what it felt like to hold her, kiss and caress her. She'd been untutored but very responsive and he discovered that his willpower where she was concerned seemed to be slipping badly.

They checked into a hotel that was considerably different in atmosphere from Vienna. They were greeted with suspicion and almost open disdain.

By the time they reached their room, Lauren could no longer control her trembling.

Jordan locked the door behind the man who had escorted them to their room, then turned to Lauren. She was looking around the room as though trying to see the surveillance equipment. He smiled. She was very brave in so many ways. Perhaps it was the non-activity of the ride that had given her too much time to think about what they would be dealing with in an iron curtain country.

"Well, my dear," he said in a hearty voice, "We're finally here. Aren't you glad we came?"

She looked around at him as though he'd lost his mind.

He walked over and put his arms around her. He could feel how stiff she was. He mouthed the words "answer me."

"Oh, yes, darling. Of course I'm glad. Just a little tired after the drive, that's all."

"Don't you want to explore the city with me, since we're here?"

She knew they had to start looking as quickly as possible. Lauren forced herself to smile. "Sounds like fun."

He smiled and pantomimed the words "good girl," then leaned down and kissed her. He'd meant it to be a reassuring kind of kiss—one that a father, brother or uncle could have given her.

However, when she responded without any restraint, Jordan forgot all his pure motives—the multitude of pep talks he'd given himself—and accepted her wholehearted cooperation by indulging in a thorough exploration of Lauren's delectable mouth.

His tongue invaded and was greeted eagerly by hers in a love play that was intensely provocative. When he finally paused for much-needed air they were both breathing hard, trying to get their bearings.

"Are you trying to distract me?" he muttered in a barely audible tone.

She grinned. "If I am, how am I doing?"

"You're asking for trouble, you know that, don't you?"

"And if I am?"

He heard the flippancy in her tone and saw the vulnerability in her eyes. Could it be possible? Was she falling for him? Dear Lord, he didn't need that. Especially now, not when they were in such a risky situation. There was no denying there was something between them. Something that would have to be worked out. Jordan knew that he wasn't going to be able to walk away from this woman and forget her.

But now wasn't the time to deal with the potentially explosive response they were having toward each other.

Jordan hugged her to him. "I didn't drive all this way to spend all our time in bed," he said in a mock-ferocious tone for the benefit of anyone who might be listening. He rubbed his knuckles along her cheek, loving the velvety softness, wishing he could touch her all over, from her ears to her toes, exploring, initiating, loving her.

Loving her? Where had that idea come from? Love was such a myth and yet, Jordan couldn't identify the strong emotion that had sprung up within him since he'd been with Lauren. He'd never felt anything like it before. As much as he wanted to make love to her he was much more concerned about her safety. He wanted to protect her from all harm.

"Let's go," he said gruffly, taking her hand and leading her from the room.

They spent the afternoon as typical tourists. They found some people who were willing to chat with them, which gave Lauren a chance to brush up on the language. Jordan watched with pride as Lauren's friendliness won over the suspicious natures of the strangers. From what Jordan could make out, she talked to them about her grandmother, mentioned some of the songs she'd been taught to sing as a child, did a few dance steps and before long was involved in a laughing discussion of the different cultures.

After some involved tracking, they also managed to locate the man who might be able to help them. When they finally found him, he was in a small room behind a local shop. He stood when Jordan walked in and then grabbed Jordan around the shoulders, hugging him tightly.

"It is good to see you once again, Jordan," he said in fluent English.

"It's good to see you, too, Stefan," Jordan replied. He'd had his arm around Lauren's waist when they came in, but had dropped it when Stefan greeted him so exuberantly. Now he turned to Lauren and, taking her hand, drew her forward. "I'd like you to meet my wife, Lauren."

Stefan laughed. "But of course, my friend. You would only have such a beautiful woman as your wife, would you not? I am so very pleased to meet you." He stuck out his hand and she grasped it gently. "Aahhh. You are very shy, I can tell."

Lauren could feel her cheeks burning and heard Jordan laugh. "There are times when she isn't so shy, Stefan," he said with a grin.

He'd almost sounded like a husband, Lauren thought with a sense of wonder. That tone of possessive pride had sounded authentic.

"Sit down, sit, both of you," Stefan exclaimed. "I must apologize for meeting you like this, but you see, I must be very careful who I am seen talking to."

"Thank you for going to all the trouble to arrange this," Jordan replied. "I appreciate it."

"I had no choice because I wanted very much to see you once again and know that things are well for you." He glanced at Lauren with a smile. "I'm pleased that you are so obviously happy." Stefan sat opposite them with a bright expression. Then the smile faded. "But you are here for more than a friendly visit, I know."

"I'm afraid so, Stefan. Have you heard anything about the disappearance of an American woman in Vienna a few days ago?"

Stefan studied the floor for a few moments of silence, then glanced up. "A nice looking woman, tall, slender, with reddish-colored hair?"

"You've seen her?" Jordan demanded eagerly.

"No, but I have heard of something that did not ring exactly true."

"What?"

"There is a story circulating about a woman who had been traveling and became ill. She was taken to a private clinic on the outskirts of town, but none of the regular employees has been allowed to care for her. She has her own nurse and doctor."

"That could be her," Jordan said thoughtfully. "Is there any way we can get in to see her?"

"We?"

"I would need to take Lauren with me."

"I see. Well, of course I can't say without doing some checking. No doubt it would be difficult, but perhaps not impossible."

Jordan laughed. "With you, Stefan, nothing is ever impossible."

"You are too kind, my friend. Give me some time and I will get back in touch with you."

"Where can I meet you?"

"I'll leave a message here at the shop by noon tomorrow. We'll see what we can do."

Jordan's frown of concentration on the way back to the hotel kept Lauren silent. He pulled up in front of a shop that sold hats, gloves and scarves and said, "Wait here. I won't be but a few minutes."

He was as good as his word. When he returned he handed her a package.

"What is this?"

"A hat with a wide brim. You'll need to wear it if we get to go into the clinic."

"You've come up with a plan, haven't you?" she asked quietly.

"I'm still debating it, but it may work." He hadn't started the car. Instead he sat gripping the wheel tightly and staring down the street. Lauren studied his grim profile.

"Tell me," she prodded.

He looked over at her and sighed. "God, I hate to get you involved in this."

"I'm already involved. You know that."

"Yes."

"So what do you have in mind?"

"I can't risk removing Mrs. Monroe—if it is Mrs. Monroe—from the clinic without causing all kinds of disturbances. The minute she's gone they'll be watching the borders for her."

Lauren nodded, understanding what he was having trouble putting into words.

"So I'll be there in her place," she said calmly.

"It's the only thing I've come up with so far, but it needs some work."

"I think it's excellent. She can leave as me. The two of you can check out of the hotel and drive back across at your leisure. If my hair and makeup is as accurate as Mr. Mallory planned, there should be no problem at all recrossing the border."

"Yes, that's what Mallory was counting on. But it leaves you in the hands of whoever kidnapped Frances Monroe."

"I know," she said quietly.

"I'm not sure I can do that."

"You don't have any choice. After all, that was the whole idea of my coming with you."

Jordan let go of the steering wheel and pounded his fist softly against it. "I don't like it."

"I'm not all that thrilled myself, you know."

"I'll talk to Stefan tomorrow, see if he has any other ideas."

"Perhaps he could help me leave the clinic later."

"As soon as I can get Mrs. Monroe to safety, I'll be back."

"But you can't. You'll be endangering—"

"The hell I can't. If I leave you, I'll damned well be back to get you."

"But we can't cross the border—"

"Not legally, but we can get across."

"Jordan, I'm sure Mr. Mallory wouldn't want you risking—"

"I don't really care what Mallory wants at this point. He's the one who recruited you for this little drama. He can accept the fact that it won't be over until you're home safely where you belong."

Lauren studied him thoughtfully. Of course she was scared. Why shouldn't she be? She had known that what she would be doing would be dangerous. As soon as they had suggested that she might be substituted for Frances Monroe, Lauren knew that she might be discovered and arrested as a spy.

There was no reason to consider that aspect of the situation. Not yet. Surely among the three of them they could devise a workable scenario with the least amount of risk for everyone concerned.

She could feel Jordan's anger and frustration radiating from him, but it was different from the day in Mr. Mallory's office. He was concerned for her because he cared about her. She understood very well. Thinking of all the dangers inherent in his crossing the border with a substitute wife caused her mind to flinch from the possibility of failure.

Jordan started the car and they drove back to the hotel in silence.

Six

They ate at the hotel in an almost empty dining room. Neither of them had much to say. Their minds were on what they might be facing the next day and they knew the discussion was over for now.

By the time they returned to the room, it was dark. Without saying anything, Lauren reached into their shared suitcase for her gown and realized that she had brought one of the silk and lace ones that were part of her role. She shrugged. When she'd packed, she'd been thinking about how things would appear at customs, not about how she'd feel actually wearing the gown. She hadn't even brought her robe.

She walked into the bathroom and filled the tub with water, grateful for the steam that told her it was hot. Shedding her clothes she gingerly crawled into the warm water and sank down with a satisfied sigh.

What a day she'd had. She'd been awakened by an explosion; then she had participated in an emotional upheaval that had destroyed all the preconceived ideas she'd had about men and sex and her own involvement in intimacies before marriage.

She continued to enumerate the events of her day in her mind: a trip behind the iron curtain, a meeting with Stefan and a plan that might mean she'd never see her homeland again. *Don't think that way!* she scolded herself. The plan would work because they would make it work. Depending on how closely she resembled Frances Monroe, it was possible Lauren could continue the charade for days.

Then what?

Jordan would be back to get her.

She smiled at the thought. She knew he would help her. Lauren had complete trust in him.

By the time she was out of the tub, Lauren felt relaxed and rested, all the minor aches and pains of travel having disappeared. After slipping on the gown she moved to the mirror and began to brush her hair.

Suddenly Lauren stopped. Her hand clenched the brush in midair, her gaze fixed on the woman in the mirror. The gown was mostly satin and it clung to her figure like a second skin. She could see the indentation of her waist just below her ribs and above her hip bones. There was even a shadow where her navel was.

She might as well be nude. In fact, her breasts were exposed through the fine lace that formed thin straps and widened slightly into two strips to her waist. She was expected to share a bed with Jordan Trent undressed like this?

She grinned. He wouldn't stand a chance.

Whatever happened tomorrow, she had tonight and she fully intended to share it with Jordan. Ever since the abrupt interruption of their lovemaking that morning the tension between them had been almost visible. Surely he didn't expect to share that bed with her and sleep! Not after this morning.

Lauren opened the door and walked out of the bathroom.

A small lamp by the bed was the room's only illumination. Jordan stood in a darkened corner staring out the window. When she walked into the room he didn't look around and from the expression on his face, his thoughts were far from pleasant.

"Jordan?"

He glanced around and suddenly straightened, his eyes locking on her as though he had no control over them.

"Yes?" he asked gruffly.

"I'm sorry for taking so long in the tub." She walked over to where he stood, the soft light now at her back.

He watched her approach him and knew there was no way he was going to be able to resist her tonight. No way. He was too worried, too fearful for her. And now she appeared in a gown he'd never seen before.

What had happened to the demure nightshirt she'd had on the night before?

Not that it would have influenced his reaction to her now, even if she wore sackcloth.

He cleared his throat. "No problem," he muttered, sidestepping her and going into the other room.

He firmly closed the door—but not before she saw the hot desire burning in his eyes and the way his body reacted to the sight of her.

She'd learned a great deal about him this morning. Lauren intended to learn even more before the night was over.

When Jordan stepped out of the bathroom after a long, invigorating shower, the bedroom yielded no light to guide him to bed. Only a faint glow from the two windows enabled him to cautiously move to where he thought the bed was.

He'd been wishing he'd brought something to sleep in. At the time he'd packed, he'd been too angry to think of all of the ramifications of traveling with a woman who was supposed to be his wife. Therefore, the only things he had to wear were dress trousers and a pair of his jeans. Neither were appropriate. Both would be damned uncomfortable.

He touched the side of the bed with his leg. Carefully feeling along the edge he came to the bedside table located near the headboard. Jordan gingerly lowered himself on the side of the bed. So far, so good. Maybe she was already asleep. He forced himself to quieten his own breathing and listen. As he gradually calmed himself he located her soft breathing nearby. If its rapid rate was any indication, she was far from asleep.

What, after all, had he expected?

At least the night before they'd had separate beds, even though they'd been within touching distance of each other. Tonight there was no pretense. They needed to sleep as a married couple. Unseen ears would be alert to anything unusual.

Besides, there wasn't even a comfortable chair in the room, much less a couch. He refused to consider trying to sleep on the floor.

Carefully lifting the covers, Jordan crawled in, making sure he kept a solid distance between himself and the center of the bed. It was going to be a long night, but he needed as much sleep as possible. Forcing himself to relax, Jordan stretched out over the length of the bed.

"Jordan, darling?"

Her sudden remark in the darkened room almost caused him to spring straight up in the bed. It was soft and seductive and from the endearment she had added, Lauren obviously knew there might be listeners.

"Hmmm?" he responded warily. What was she up to?

"I never did ask you. Do you mind if this one turns out to be a girl?"

An electrified silence filled the room after her question. He whipped his head around on the pillow but couldn't see anything but a faint silhouette of her body.

"What?" he asked in a strangled voice.

"You know, the baby," she said in a tone that told him she was smiling. "I know we didn't plan on starting our family this soon, but you aren't sorry now that this one's on the way... are you?" she asked wistfully.

"Uh, Lauren—"

He felt her shift in the bed. Her foot slid along his ankle and rubbed against his arch. Jordan almost jackknifed out of the bed at her touch. "What are you doing!" he demanded in a harsh whisper.

"Oh, I'm sorry, love. Am I crowding you? This is considerably smaller than our bed back home, isn't it?" she said. "But then we never have taken up much room when we're together." She edged closer so that her hair brushed against his shoulder. "I hope he looks like you," she added.

"Who?"

"The baby. If it's a boy I'd like to name him after you. I hope his hair is black and curly like yours, and that he has large black eyes and your mischievous grin."

"Mischievous—" Jordan broke off at the thought of Lauren having his baby. For a moment he could see the infant she was describing as clearly as if it were there in the room with them: the black curly hair, the smile. Only the eyes were gray, wide pools of early morning mist staring back at him.

Then a little girl joined the baby. She had curls, too, but hers were a sandy red, almost carrot topped, her eyes a deep brown. She held up her hands to him as though expecting him to take her.

Jordan shook his head, blinking several times. Was he losing his mind? Was the stress too much? He'd been right. He was too old for this sort of life. He needed to be put away in some peaceful sanitarium somewhere—

"Or would you rather we name him after your father?"

Without conscious thought, Jordan responded. "No. I don't want to name him after my father." His voice sounded harsh in the quiet room and he tried to cover his reaction. "How about naming him after your father?" When he heard himself speak, only then did Jordan face the fact that he was going along with her idiotic game.

"Matthew Mackenzie Trent. It does have a nice ring to it, doesn't it?" she said with a certain amount of pride.

Jordan grinned. She certainly sounded like a proud mama introducing her son to an adoring audience. He shifted by turning over on his side and felt her from his shoulder down to his toes. Casually sliding his knee across her, he let his hand drop lightly on her chest, cupping her breast.

"What about our daughter?" he asked, while beginning to nibble on her exposed ear. Jordan could feel her heart racing in her chest. Surprised that she could sound so casually sleepy with a heart pounding like a steam engine, Jordan wondered just how far she intended to carry out her little game.

"Our daughter?" she repeated, ending on a breathless note.

"Umhmmm…" he replied, planting a row of kisses down her neck and lightly touching the pulsing beat at the base of her throat with his tongue. "Just in case it's a girl."

"Oh! Well, uh, I'm not sure."

"She'll probably have your color hair and your large eyes that seem to fill a man with all kinds of ideas—"

"They do? I mean—"

"Oh, yes. If we weren't already married I definitely would have been irritated at the way some of those men were looking at you today."

"But I—"

He cut off whatever she was going to say by the simple means of placing his mouth over hers. She tried to move away only to find herself held firmly by his arm and leg across her.

Not that Lauren wanted to move away. Not exactly, anyway. She just hadn't expected him to pounce quite so suddenly. She'd been lying there thinking about how little they could talk about in the room. One thought had led to another and she had decided to tease him. Just a little. But he'd turned it back on her without effort.

Funny, but she could see both a baby boy and a little girl. They were happy children, laughing, filled with love—and she felt such a fierce tug of joy that she turned toward him, holding him close. He'd probably only meant the kiss to shut her up, but now that she was where she'd wanted to be all along...

Jordan felt her resistance fade away and she flowed against him. Her breasts nudged his chest and she shifted her leg so that she sandwiched his knee between her thighs.

All of his good intentions deserted him at that moment. He certainly wasn't a saint, even though he'd tried to be one. And Lauren wasn't helping him at all. If he didn't know better, he'd swear she was intent on seducing him.

He leaned up on his elbow and looked down at her shadowy face. With a wicked smile he exaggerated a yawn and said, ''Well, darlin', it's been a long day. Guess we should try to get some rest. You especially need to take good care of yourself,'' he added. At the same time he began to slide first one of her gown straps off her shoulder, then the other.

Lauren made a strangled sound that was something between a cough and a gasp. Jordan continued to tug at her gown until it was around her waist. ''Goodnight,'' he said just before he began to kiss her.

His kisses were filled with passion and determination. There was no doubt in either of their minds that this time he would make love to her and that she would not discourage him.

Ever conscious of their need to be quiet, Jordan's silent lovemaking touched Lauren with his gentleness. While his hands softly brushed the silk and lace down off her body until the gown lay around her feet, his mouth continued to explore her. Her silky skin drew him on to touch and taste her. At one point he was aware that she put her fist to her mouth rather than allow a moan to escape.

She had tantalized and teased him, even if it hadn't been intentional. Now there was no turning back. Before morning, Lauren Mackenzie would better understand the intimate relationship between a man and a woman.

Lauren began to imitate what Jordan was doing, with remarkable results. When she brushed her hand across his abdomen, his stomach muscles rippled with reaction. She came into contact with the waist line of his briefs and, following his example, began to slide them down his muscular thighs and calves.

Moving very slowly so that the bed barely shifted, Jordan rolled over until he was on top of Lauren. She felt his weight pressing her down for a brief moment, then he rested on his forearms. "Am I too heavy?" he whispered almost inaudibly in her ear. She shook her head in answer.

He found her mouth once more, teasing her with nibbling little kisses across her bottom lip, tracing the line of her upper lip with his tongue, until his actions got to both of them. Suddenly penetrating her mouth with his tongue, he began to show her what he intended to do with her, his lazy strokes allowing her an opportunity to draw away if she wished.

Instead Lauren pulled him closer, shifting slightly to accommodate his weight. By the time he rose slightly above her, they were both trembling with need and desire. Lauren had never guessed that lovemaking could be so beautiful, such a luscious sharing of another person. She knew that she would be forever thankful that she had found Jordan and had the opportunity to get to know him. Having him show her the mysterious art of lovemaking seemed to be what she had waited for all her life.

Jordan lowered himself with slow deliberation until she fully sheathed him. How had he ever lived this long without experiencing such an awe-inspiring sensation of oneness with another person? He held her close to him without moving, savoring the delightful intensity of the moment.

Lauren smiled into the darkness, clutching him to her, her head sheltered in his shoulder. This was wonderful. She had expected pain, or at the very least discomfort. Instead she was astonished at his patience in seeking entrance, moving so slowly that he gave her body an opportunity to adjust to him.

His exaggeratedly slow movements were extremely erotic for them both. Constantly aware of a certain lack of privacy, Jordan was determined to give her pleasure without feeling that others were getting a vicarious thrill from their lovemaking.

The silence of the room lay unbroken except for an occasional sigh or the soft sound of a sheet being shifted, all of which could be explained as the sounds made by restless people trying to sleep in a new bed in a strange country.

Lauren felt as though something deep inside of her was becoming unraveled; the more it loosened and moved the more tense she became. Her body felt as though it were on the brink of exploding; tiny fingers of bright lights and colors seemed to shimmer in the darkness. Abruptly a shower of fireworks appeared to burst all around her, filling the room with radiance and joy, hope and love.

She buried her head deeply into his chest and held on. Jordan gave one strong surge of movement that seemed to set off a shudder that raced from his head down to his toes. Lauren felt his arms quivering, then he lowered himself helplessly to the bed beside her, his breathing harsh.

Pulling her to him he held her as though he never intended to let her go. She was content to fall asleep that way.

Sometime during the night Lauren awoke to the most marvelous sensations. Jordan still held her in his arms while he touched her delicately with his hands and mouth.

His lovemaking seemed to be a part of her dream-like state and she responded to him mindlessly, knowing that their time together would end in a few hours.

The next time she awakened, Jordan was saying in a normal speaking voice, "Time to get up, darling, if we're going to get any sight-seeing done."

Lauren blinked open her eyes, squinting in the harsh light. She managed to focus on Jordan who stood by the side of the bed. The shock of seeing him standing there nude woke her quicker than a pail of ice water dumped on the bed.

She let out a gasp and pulled up the covers to her shoulders.

It was one thing to make passionate love to a man in the dark. It was something else to see that man in all of his natural splendor. Then she realized he was totally unconcerned with his lack of adornment.

"I thought it might save us some time if we showered together," he said nonchalantly, with a decidedly wicked look in his eyes.

"Oh, but, I, uh—"

He began a steady pressure, pulling the sheet from her nerveless fingers. "Come on, honey. We need to get a move on." Reaching down he grasped her hands and pulled her to her feet, glancing down at her with a smile. He began to walk her to the bathroom. "How did you sleep last night, dear?"

"Oh! Well, I didn't seem to—"

"I know. A strange bed and all. It's hard to get enough rest when you travel. I've spent so many years on the road that I've grown used to it."

Lauren had never known that she was capable of blushing all over. One glance into the mirror of the bathroom convinced her it was possible. Her face blushed an even brighter shade of red when she discovered that he wasn't unaffected by her.

He leaned over and kissed her under the ear, then slid his arms around her. They both stood facing the mirror. His expression reflected his amusement at her embarrassment.

"If you think I'm about to apologize for what happened last night, you're in for quite a shock," he said in a low voice.

She shook her head but somehow couldn't find her voice. Pulling her under the steady stream of water with him, he systematically soaped her entire body with loving caresses until Lauren forgot about her embarrassment. Now she could study the body that she'd only explored by touch last night. She had to admit there was something to be said for the braille method of learning, but she enjoyed being able to see him as well.

Lauren's body seemed to have learned some amazing responses to him in a very short while. Either that, or he knew what buttons to push to cause a strong reaction from deep within her.

When he lifted her, coaxing her to wrap her legs around his waist, she gasped out loud.

"Am I hurting you?" he asked, a slight frown pulling his brows together.

She shook her head.

"You can talk to me, you know. We've got the water running."

Lauren was too stunned by feeling to be able to think of anything to say. "Isn't this going to hurt your back?" she finally managed to gasp.

He kissed her—a long, drugging, possessive kiss that wiped the question from her mind. When he finally raised his head she felt so weak she could barely hold on to him.

"Are you going to give me a rubdown if I do hurt my back?" he asked in a mischievous tone of voice. "If so, it might be worth it."

She could no longer concentrate on his teasing. Lauren arched her back and let out a small cry and felt as though she were melting.

Jordan gave a convulsive movement, clasping her so close she could hardly get her breath. After a few moments he slowly lowered her to her feet.

"Wow!" he managed to say when he could catch his breath.

"Wow? What's that supposed to mean?"

"Wow! You're a pretty potent bathing partner."

She grinned, suddenly feeling extremely pleased with herself. Jordan acted as though she'd known what she was doing to him, when all the time she'd been following his lead.

Gingerly crawling out of the shower, she discovered that her knees were shaking so hard she could hardly stand. "I'm not so sure that was a good idea," she said huskily.

Leaving the water running, Jordan was out of the shower with his arms around her asking, "What's wrong? I did hurt you, didn't I? Damn!"

She shook her head. "I just didn't have any idea— How could I have known—" She glanced into the mirror and saw his anxious expression. "I'm all right, really," she said, managing to put a little stiffening into her knees. "I didn't mean to scare you."

"Oh, Lauren," he said, burying his face in her hair. "I would never want to hurt you."

"I know," she responded softly. If she got hurt over this relationship, she would have no one but herself to blame. She'd made the decision and she wasn't sorry. Now they had to get on with why they were there.

Reaching for a towel, she said, "Shouldn't you turn off the water before someone checks to see if we have a leak in this room?"

Jordan nodded without saying anything. He just released her and leaned into the shower and turned off the water.

"So what's on the agenda today?" she asked in a casual voice.

He followed her into the bedroom and they began to dress. Lauren couldn't keep her eyes off him, but she tried very hard not to stare.

"You remember the little curio shop we found yesterday?" he asked and she knew he was talking about the place where they'd met Stefan.

"Oh, yes."

"I keep thinking about that chess set I saw in there, with all the hand carved pieces. That would be a great gift for your dad, don't you think?"

She grinned. "Absolutely." *If my dad knew anything about chess, that is.* "I'm pleased you thought of him," she added.

He walked over and adjusted the collar of her dress, then allowed his hand to slide slowly down to her waist, then back up. "Oh, I always think of your family. They're great people. Did you remember to buy postcards to send to Meg and Amy?"

Lauren gave him a sharp look and caught the teasing glint in his eye. "Well, I thought you'd prefer to wait until we get to France to purchase those. You know how my sisters are."

His brows shot up and she flashed him a very innocent look.

Jordan glanced at his watch. "I suppose we should get going. We overslept a little this morning."

"Oh, well, what difference does it make, anyway? We're on vacation." She picked up her purse and the hat he'd bought her the day before.

"Glad you reminded me. I keep trying to keep some sort of schedule."

Stefan had a message waiting for them when they arrived at the little shop. They were to meet him at three o'clock by a well-known landmark of the city. Jordan suggested lunch, since they weren't sure when they might get another opportunity to eat.

He kept studying her during their meal until she became self-conscious. "What's the matter, do I have dirt on my face?"

If anything, Jordan's expression merely became more intent. "No. You've just surprised me, that's all," he finally said, slowly taking a bite of his neglected meal.

"You didn't realize how aggressive I was going to be, perhaps?" She tried for flippancy but from his expression, he wasn't buying it.

"I'd like to understand why," he said thoughtfully, as though repeating something that had run through his head several times.

"Why?" she repeated hesitantly.

"Why me? Why now? Why wait this long in your life and then make such a decision?"

"Are you saying I should have sat down and figured all of this out on a logical basis before making love to you?"

"I'm saying," he repeated in a patiently level tone, "that you acted totally out of character and you know it."

"You don't know my character all that well, obviously."

"I know I was the first man you'd ever been with."

"My inexperience showed, huh? And here I thought I learned so quickly."

"And you aren't fooling me for a minute, Lauren. From everything I've discovered about you, I know you to be a strong, independent woman who doesn't do anything on impulse."

"You've got to be kidding. This whole trip is an impulse. What if I just said that I was tired of my old life-style and wanted a change of pace?"

"Why me?"

She couldn't bring herself to carry on the brittle comments any longer; couldn't force herself to say, "Because you were available."

Playing for time, she took a sip from her glass, then set it down in front of her. Raising her chin slightly, she met his intent gaze. "Maybe I fell in love with you."

She watched him flinch as though she'd slapped him and knew she shouldn't be surprised. What had she expected, anyway?

"You know there's no future in it," he said quietly.

"I know."

"My life-style is—"

"I'm quite aware of your life-style. Please don't draw me any pictures, okay?"

"I took advantage of the situation after I told you—"

"Why do you have to take all the credit? I managed to take a few advantages myself, you know."

He shook his head, not at all pleased with the way the conversation was going. Wouldn't she take anything seriously?

Of course she didn't love him. What a joke. She didn't even like him. And who could blame her, the way he'd treated her from the very beginning. And yet there was something—something between them that showered sparks all around whenever they were near each other. Even after the past several hours of making love to her, Jordan recognized that he wanted her again. What was it about her that affected him so?

He wished to hell he knew.

Glancing at his watch he said, "We've got to go." Jordan signaled the waiter and when he'd brought their check, quickly paid the bill. Then he took Lauren's hand and they walked out of the restaurant together, that peculiar radiance that lovers seem to reflect obvious to everyone who glanced their way.

Seven

They circled the park twice like a couple enjoying the view and the day. Jordan teased her, whispering in her ear and making her blush, meanwhile unobtrusively watching for Stefan. Even so, he didn't recognize him.

An elderly man with a slight limp, using a cane, nodded as they passed him. It took Jordan a few seconds to remember when he'd last seen that old man. He began to laugh.

"What's so funny?"

"I forgot about Stefan's love for disguises."

She glanced around the park. "Where is he?"

"Never mind. We'll find a bench and sit down in a moment. I'm sure he'll join us."

After fifteen minutes or so, they were joined on the park bench by the same elderly man who nodded to them once again. Jordan continued to look and speak to Lauren; however his speech was directed past her shoulder. "You could have at least warned me this was going to be a costume party."

"No problem," the man muttered, as though talking to himself. "Thought you'd recognize the outfit."

"Any word?"

"Yes. The information we have is correct."

"Can we get in there?"

The old man fished into his pocket and pulled out a small bag of peanuts. He tossed one on the ground and watched a squirrel scurry from a nearby tree, grab the nut and race back to safety.

"It will be a little risky, but yes."

"How?"

Jordan continued to smile and play with the curl in front of Lauren's ear, but his eyes were watching the man nearby.

"I have made arrangements for the nurse to meet with her lover for a few minutes around five o'clock. That is still during visiting hours. You and your wife will go as visitors, mingling until you get inside. I've drawn a map which is inside the newspaper lying here beside me. Once in the clinic you will need to slip into the other wing. Her room is marked. You won't have long."

"What sort of condition is she in?"

"They couldn't give me anything on that."

"If I leave Lauren there until I can get the woman out of the country, how much protection can you give Lauren?"

"Whatever is necessary."

Jordan realized he'd been barely breathing until that last remark. Even so, their plan might not work. But if they could get to Mrs. Monroe, they'd have more information and a better chance of deciding what to do.

"Will we see you?"

"I'll be there, but you won't see me," Stefan said to a scampering squirrel.

Jordan leaned over and kissed Lauren. "We'll be there at five," he said as he pulled away from her. He picked up the paper and stuck it under his arm in an absent manner. Taking her hand, he pulled her to her feet, for all the world like a lover who was anxious to find someplace private.

Neither of them looked back at the elderly man who continued to sit and toss peanuts at the squirrels.

Jordan was pleased to see enough people going in and out of the clinic that he and Lauren could easily blend into the crowd. He'd had Lauren wear the hat he'd purchased the day before, just in case. It completely shadowed her face.

Once inside, they followed the hallway until it turned. Then they found the stairwell and went up two flights, down another hallway until they reached the end. Praying that Stefan's plan still worked, Jordan tried the door on room 301. It opened. He peered inside. The drapes were drawn and it was shadowy but he could faintly see a woman in the only bed in the room.

Tugging at Lauren's hand, he pulled her inside and closed the door. Walking quietly over to the bed, he said, "Mrs. Monroe?"

The woman's head turned toward him.

"Are you Frances Monroe?"

She licked her lips and nodded. "Yes," she tried to say, as though unused to talking. "Who are you?" she managed to whisper, her voice breaking.

Jordan reached for her hand lying on the cover. "Your husband sent me, Mrs. Monroe. I'm going to get you out of here."

"Trevor?" Her voice grew stronger and she struggled to sit up. "Trevor's here? Oh, thank God. This nightmare's over."

"Shhhh, we don't have much time and we're going to need your help."

She nodded her head. "Yes. Whatever. Just tell me."

"Can you walk all right?"

"I'm not sure. They've been keeping me so doped up. I seem to have lost track of the days. They've been running together." Her voice became stronger. "Of course I can walk. I'll do whatever I have to."

Jordan patted her hand and spoke to Lauren. "Quick. Get out of that dress and hat." Then to Mrs. Monroe he explained, "Lauren is going to stay here in your place for a few hours. Just long enough to get you out of the country."

"But they'll see her and know—"

"Not as long as the room stays dark. If they turn on a light she can protest." He spoke as much for Lauren as for Frances Monroe.

Lauren realized that the moment of truth had arrived. It was time to do what she had to do, regardless of how frightened she was. Getting Mrs. Monroe safely back was the only thing that counted now. She stripped down to her panties and bra, then looked at Jordan inquiringly.

"Mrs. Monroe, I'm going to turn my back while you slip out of that gown and into these clothes, okay?" he asked gently.

Frances nodded. He could see that her hands were trembling so much that she would have trouble dressing herself. Fortunately Lauren stepped forward and began to help her.

When Frances stood up, Lauren was grateful to see that they were of a similar height and build. Thank God they'd gotten that much of the situation right. She couldn't see Frances's hair color, but the length was similar to hers.

"What color are your eyes?" Lauren asked.

Puzzled, the woman said, "Blue. Why?"

"Mine are gray. That's close enough."

"What do you mean?"

"You're going to be using my passport to get out of here."

"But how will you get out?" Frances asked, alarmed by the suddenness of what was happening.

Jordan spoke from across the room. "I should have you with your husband in a few hours, Mrs. Monroe. Then I'm coming back for Lauren."

Lauren hurriedly pulled Frances's gown over her head and slipped into the bed. Frances placed Lauren's hat on her head. "You can turn around now,"

Frances said. When he did, she said, "I never even asked your name."

"Jordan. Jordan Trent. I'm a great admirer of your husband, Mrs. Monroe. He doesn't need this kind of pressure on him."

She nodded. "I know. I've been so worried for him. There was no way to get word to him."

"Have they treated you all right?"

"Yes. I've only seen three people. The two men who stopped the car there in Vienna, and then the woman who stays here with me. How did you know she'd be gone?"

"We hoped. Look, we've got to go." He glanced over at Lauren who had stretched out on the bed in the same pose they'd found Frances Monroe in. He leaned over and gave her a hard kiss. "Don't worry. I'll be back soon."

She nodded. "I know."

Opening the door slightly, Jordan peered out. "Ready?" he asked, glancing back at Frances.

She nodded and followed him out of the room.

Lauren lay there forcing herself to take deep breaths. She needed to stay calm. Stefan was somewhere nearby. He would protect her. And before long, Jordan would be back for her.

She had to believe that. She couldn't afford to think of the many possibilities that could change all of their plans.

By the time they reached the main floor, Frances was shaking so hard she could hardly walk. "I'm sorry," she gasped. "But I've been in bed for days. I hadn't realized how weak I'd become."

Jordan wrapped his arm around her waist. "We're fine. Pretend you're overcome with grief. Keep your head down and we'll walk slowly to the car."

"Then what do we do?"

"Go back to the hotel, pack and get out of here."

He nodded to several people who passed them, looking at Frances's lowered head in concern.

"You're doing just fine," he murmured. "Don't be surprised when I call you Lauren."

"She's very brave to be doing this."

"Yes, she is."

"How fortunate that we could exchange clothes," she said breathlessly, "although I'm having a little trouble keeping the shoes on."

He grinned. "That's better than if they were too small."

He felt more than heard her slight chuckle. "Yes."

Their murmured conversation got them past the lobby and outside the front door. Both of them took a deep breath.

"I've had no idea where I was."

"Don't you remember coming here?"

"It was night. And I was so frightened. I was so afraid they were going to try to hurt Trevor through me."

An amazing woman, Jordan acknowledged to himself. How many women in her position would have been worrying over their husband?

Lauren would, if she were placed in a similar position.

He wasn't sure where the thought had come from, but recognized the truth of it. The similarity between the two women was more than superficial.

Frances dozed during the trip to the hotel and apologized when he woke her up after they'd arrived. "I can't seem to stay awake."

"Don't worry about it. You're doing fine." He helped her out of the car and into the hotel. He took her immediately to the room. Once inside, he said, "Why don't you lie down, darling, and see if that helps?" When she glanced up at him with a startled expression, he placed his finger to his lips, lifted the hat off her head and motioned for her to lie down.

Glancing around the room Frances nodded and laid down.

Jordan picked up the phone and rang the front desk. When someone answered, he said, "This is Jordan Trent. I'm afraid my wife must have eaten something that didn't agree with her. She's decided she wants to go back to Vienna tonight rather than to continue our sight-seeing. I'd appreciate it if you'd have our bill ready in a few minutes." He listened to an explanation. "Of course I understand. No. There's no problem. I'm sure it's nothing serious. Yes. We've had a very pleasant stay."

As soon as he hung up, Jordan went into the bathroom and quickly gathered up their toiletry articles.

When he walked back into the room he noticed that Frances had closed her eyes once again. In the clear light coming from the window he could see that she was a very nice-looking woman. The dress, indeed, looked like one she might have chosen. Her fair skin and goldish-red hair were remarkably similar to Lauren's, but she didn't affect him in the same way.

How strange. They were enough alike to pass as sisters, and yet one of them increased his pulse rate just by being in the same room with him, and the other one had no effect on him whatsoever.

What was it that caused the chemistry between people? He'd never had a reaction to a woman such as he did to Lauren. He didn't understand it at all.

At the moment he didn't have time to seek any answers, either. He tossed the items from the bathroom into the suitcase and closed it.

After he double-checked the room to be sure he'd packed all of their belongings, he walked over to the bed. "Lauren?"

Frances's eyes flew open at the sound of his voice. "Oh! I did it again."

"No problem." He helped her off the bed, picked up the suitcase and escorted her downstairs.

They were headed for the Austrian border within the hour. "I can't believe how easily you've managed all of this," Frances commented after they'd been traveling for several miles.

"It's part of my job," he said with a smile.

"What is that? Rescuing kidnap victims?"

"Among other things."

"Where is Trevor? Will he be in Vienna?"

"I'm taking you to an American military base. He intended to wait there until you were located."

"He never went home?"

Jordan glanced at her out of the corner of his eye. "What do you think?"

She smiled. "Knowing Trevor, I'm surprised he didn't come after me himself."

"I'm sure he wanted to, but no one wanted to take any chances. Actually, I believe that's what your kidnappers hoped would happen."

"What do you mean?"

"Well, I've been putting some things together. We didn't have much problem locating you. It was as though you were supposed to be found."

"Then you think they would have let me go if I'd just asked?"

"Oh, no. The only reason there's been no alarm so far is because they're still confident they're holding you." *I hope,* he added silently.

"How much longer until the border?"

"Not much longer." He explained the procedure at the border and suggested she wear the hat and work hard at looking relaxed.

"If I were any more relaxed, I'd slither off the seat," she said with a grin. "My head is swimming and I feel as though I've been on a drunken spree for days."

"When was the last time they gave you something?"

"I don't remember. I had no concept of time while I was there."

"Did it seem to be given on some sort of schedule or whenever you appeared to need it?"

"I'm not sure. I tried to be very cooperative and quiet. I didn't want to give them any excuse to use force."

A very wise lady, Jordan thought to himself.

Crossing the border between Czechoslovakia and Austria was almost anticlimactic. The car and luggage were carefully scrutinized, their passports studied, but eventually they were allowed to pass.

They had driven several miles in silence before Jordan became aware of Frances Monroe's quiet sobs. He pulled over by the side of the road and stopped.

She glanced over at him, wiping her eyes. "I'm sorry," she gulped, trying to get her breath. "I know I'm being such a baby...but I was so scared and then—" she drew another ragged breath "—when I realized we'd made it...that we're actually free, I—" She started sobbing once again.

"Mrs. Monroe, you have my permission to kick, scream and cry. You've been extremely brave about all of this, and your reaction now is not only normal, but very healthy."

He reached into his pocket and drew out a clean handkerchief, handing it to her. Then he started down the road once again.

By the time Frances Monroe reached the American base where her husband anxiously waited for her, all trace of her earlier bout of tears was gone. She looked calm and in full control of herself. The tranquilizing effects of the medicine had also disappeared. Jordan was almost amused at her jaunty step when they walked down the hallway to the area assigned to Senator Monroe.

Jordan felt very blessed to have witnessed the look on Trevor Monroe's face when he caught a glimpse of his wife for the first time in over a week. He jumped to his feet and rushed toward her. "Fran! Oh, God! I can't believe it! You're actually here!" He picked her up and swung her around, then hastily placed her back on her feet. "Are you all right, darling? My God! I've been out of my mind. I didn't know—If only I'd been with you—"

She hugged him, laughing at his practically incoherent remarks. "I'm fine, just fine. In fact, I've had a marvelous rest for the last few days in this really fancy home. They treated me like a princess." She smiled at his look of disbelief. "Really." She placed her hand over her heart. "Would I lie to you?" she asked.

"If you thought you'd get away with it, yes!" he said emphatically. He glanced over at Jordan for the first time, as though only now becoming aware that Frances was not alone.

"Are you Trent?" the senator asked, walking over with his hand out.

"Yes," Jordan replied, taking the proffered hand.

Trevor Monroe nodded. "Mallory said you could pull it off. Damned if he wasn't right." He shook Jordan's hand. "You definitely deserve a raise out of this one, and I'll strongly recommend it."

"Actually, an uninterrupted vacation would be a really nice gesture."

Trevor smiled, the strain of the past few days seeming to drain away from his face. "That's right. Mallory said something about his best man being on vacation. I guess that was my fault, because I demanded the best."

Jordan shrugged. "I was glad to be of some assistance."

The senator spun around and went back to his wife. "We need to get you to the hospital and make sure you're okay. Then there are several people who will want to talk to you about what happened."

"I believe it's called 'debriefing,' isn't it?" she asked with an innocent expression on her face, unable to completely disguise her grin at his take-charge attitude.

"We'll need you, too, Trent. We've got to let them know that they can't get away with this."

"Sorry," Jordan replied, without a trace of sincerity in his voice. "Another time, perhaps. I have a little more work to do before this matter is completely cleared up."

"What do you mean?" the senator demanded to know.

"He left his wife, darling, in order to bring me across the border."

"Your wife!"

"Lauren Mackenzie," Jordan said. "She's the lady who volunteered to take your wife's place, if necessary. In the end, that plan seemed to be the most expedient one to follow."

"I didn't realize the two of you were married..."

"According to our passports, we are. As you know, it's a federal offense to falsify any information on a passport."

"So it is," the senator murmured.

"I've got to get back to her tonight, if possible."

Trevor Monroe glanced at his watch. "As late as it is, you'd be better off getting some rest before going back."

"I know, but I can't spare the time. I'm sure that nice, long vacation I'm going to get will cure all my problems in a few days," he said, and walked out of the room.

He heard the senator's laugh, pleased to know that at least one person was satisfied with the progress so far.

Jordan had a gnawing sense that he needed to get back to Lauren as quickly as possible.

Eight

Lauren lost track of time as she lay in the darkened room. She tried to keep her mind blank. There was nothing to fear. Stefan was nearby. He would not let anything happen to her. She trusted Stefan because Jordan trusted Stefan. There was no reason to panic. Everything was working exactly as planned.

When the door opened she had to force herself to keep her eyes closed and her head turned away. Lauren deliberately drew small, even breaths and waited.

The room filled with light and she realized the bedside lamp had been turned on. She threw her arm over her face and muttered, "The light's so bright."

A woman answered her in Czech to the effect that Lauren would have to get used to the light because the newcomer didn't intend to sit there in the dark!

The stranger's tone of voice had been pleasant and Lauren realized that the nurse was used to not being understood by her captive patient. Perhaps Lauren's knowledge of the language would help her if things didn't continue to progress as planned.

As her eyes adjusted to the light Lauren peered from beneath her bent arm at the woman sitting nearby. She was built like a wrestler. No wonder Mrs. Monroe hadn't made any effort to get away from here.

Lauren wasn't sure what she was going to do when she had to remove her arm. Seen up close, she bore little facial resemblance to the senator's wife. Then what would happen?

She'd rather not think about it.

Deciding that she'd better move before her arm fell off from the strained position, she turned her back to her captor and stared at the wall.

Oh, Jordan, I hope you've managed to get her away from here. We make a great team, darling, don't you think so?

Of course he didn't think so. Except for their rather passionately compatible interlude in bed, she was certain that Jordan Trent had little use for her.

She wondered when it would occur to him that they had taken no precautions during their night and morning together.

Lauren had been aware of the lack of protection at that time. The thought had given her hope that perhaps she'd become pregnant. She was fully aware of the many reasons why Jordan would never be a permanent part of her life; knew she had no choice but to accept that her time with him was limited. Having his baby would help to ease her loss.

She would still have a part of him in the years to come, someone to love and cherish when she no longer had Jordan.

Lauren knew that her family would be horrified, as strictly as she'd been brought up. And she really couldn't blame them. She could almost see the sad expression in her father's eyes. Perhaps she could make them understand. She loved Jordan. And because she loved him, she wanted his child.

It wasn't as though she didn't make enough money to care for a child. Other single parents managed. So could she.

There was a tap on the door and she almost leaped out of her skin at the sudden intrusion into the silence of the room.

The woman called out, "Who is it?" in her native language.

A man's voice answered, "Anton."

She told him to come in. A low-voiced conference took place by the door and Lauren strained her ears to hear what they were saying. A couple of names were mentioned, as well as places. She committed them to memory while she continued to listen.

There seemed to be some change of plans afoot. They intended to move her first thing in the morning. Oh dear God! What if Jordan couldn't locate her when he returned?

Don't panic, she reminded herself. *Stefan is here,* she repeated several times. Everything is under control. All I need to do is to lie quietly, pretend to be drugged, and wait.

Lauren had never been too good at waiting. She hadn't realized how nerve-racking it would be to lie there so close to Frances's captors and wait to be disclosed as an imposter.

That line of thinking would quickly reduce her to hysteria and she forced herself to think of Jordan and the night before.

That line of thinking would raise her blood pressure to dangerous levels. What she needed to do was think of something peaceful, soothing—the sounds of a babbling brook, a soft breeze sifting through the trees, the murmuring of...

Lauren fell asleep.

Jordan's return to Czechoslovakia was not through normal routes. He was pleased to see that his contacts near the border were still in place, busily making money smuggling people and goods back and forth.

By the time he left the small cottage hidden deep in the woods, near the border but well within the boundary of Czechoslovakia, even Jordan's mother wouldn't have recognized him.

His clothes were those of a common laborer and not too clean. He wore a cloth cap pulled low over his eyes. The man who had given him a lift into town gave him instructions.

"You must be back by nightfall or I can't guarantee your chances of getting across."

"I'll do what I can, Franz. I'll have a woman with me."

"Bah! Why waste so much time and go to such trouble for a woman? It would be easier to find another one."

Jordan laughed. "An interesting philosophy, but one I'm afraid I don't share."

"Women are all the same."

"You know, Franz, I have to admit that I used to feel the same way, until recently. Very recently. That's when I discovered that I could be wrong."

"Never. They cannot be trusted."

"Well, I'd trust this one with my life."

"Obviously. You're risking your life for her."

"She did the same thing for me."

"But for different reasons, you can be sure."

"What do you mean?"

"Women are devious creatures. They never say what they mean nor mean what they say."

Jordan realized he'd never be able to sway Franz from his way of thinking. Why should he try? What amazed him was how much his own way of thinking had changed since meeting Lauren.

Had he once sounded so idiotic, tagging half the human race with silly labels? How easy that was, to place names on others who are different from us in order to feel superior. He shook his head. Had he become so opinionated that others saw and heard another Franz in him? It was something to think about.

Jordan closed his eyes for a moment. They burned from lack of sleep. It was almost dawn and he was still several hours away from Brno. He had to contact Stefan. Hopefully he'd managed to get Lauren out of that room before anyone discovered the switch.

Somehow he was afraid it wouldn't be that easy.

A harsh voice spoke nearby and Lauren woke with a jerk. "Here is your food. Eat," she was told in a gruff voice. The words were supposedly English but so heavily accented as to be unrecognizable. It was only when she saw the food on a tray that she understood what had been said.

Keeping her head down, she pushed herself up on the pillow and reached for the fork.

When Lauren glanced up, she noticed with relief that the woman had already turned her back to her and sat back down with her needlework.

Lauren couldn't believe she'd been there this long and had not been discovered. But then no one had expected a switch. The plan had been brilliantly audacious. Removing Mrs. Monroe without substituting someone else would have immediately set off an alert. The longer she stayed there undetected, the better chance Jordan had of getting Frances Monroe to safety.

Lauren wondered how long it would take.

She ate as much of the food as she could, then once again turned her back and pretended to be asleep. She prayed they wouldn't bother her anymore that night.

When the light finally went out, Lauren had lost all track of time. She heard the rustling of clothes as the other woman undressed. Since there was no other bed in the room, she assumed her guardian must be sleeping on the couch across the room.

They had talked about moving her in the morning. Would Jordan be too late getting there to find her?

It was almost ten o'clock in the morning when Jordan reached Brno. He'd made good time. Franz had left him at a warehouse near the border where he'd hitched a ride with a truck driver who was making a delivery to Brno.

Franz had slipped the man some money, explaining that Jordan was too stupid to understand much of what was said to him. Jordan was pleased that he had managed to understand most of what had been said. At least the trucker wouldn't be expecting much conversation.

As soon as he was dropped off he headed for the curio shop to find Stefan. When he got there Jordan discovered that no one had seen Stefan since the day before.

Jordan didn't like the sound of that at all. He started following the route of his original contacts, working through them patiently to discover where Stefan could be found. He didn't want to blow everything wide open by showing up at the clinic dressed the way he was. No one would expect him to be visiting patients looking like that.

A hand clamped over Lauren's mouth, hard, so that she could barely breathe. She tried to struggle but her hands were easily caught and held.

The room was pitch-black. She felt as though she were in a deep well with no way out and had a horrible feeling that she was going to suffocate without ever seeing the light of day again.

Something moved by her ear and a voice whispered, "Stefan."

She relaxed, finally understanding, and the hand was immediately removed. Strong arms lifted her effortlessly from the bed and she placed her arms around Stefan's neck. He seemed to be able to see in the dark because he strode across the room and opened the door without making a sound.

The hall was dimly lit and she looked at the man who carried her. It *was* Stefan, thank God. He smiled at her while he strode down the hallway to the stairway she and Jordan had used earlier. This time he took her all the way to the basement.

"I can walk, you know," she managed to whisper as he trotted down the steps as though she were weightless.

"I didn't bring any shoes for you," he said in a low voice. "We can't afford the delay of your trying to go barefoot."

"Oh."

When Stefan opened the door into the basement, she flinched at the sudden bright light. Hiding her head against his shoulder, she waited while he hurried through the corridor and at last reached an exit.

Outside the sky was still black.

"What time is it?" she asked.

"It's almost dawn."

"Have you heard from Jordan?"

"No. But that isn't unusual. He will be in touch as soon as he can."

"Where are you taking me?"

"Out into the countryside where you will be safe."

Lauren wondered if she would ever feel safe again.

They seemed to drive for hours through dense forest. Lauren soon became lost. If anyone had been following them, they, too, would have become lost.

When Stefan pulled into the driveway of a small cottage, the sun had been up for several hours. "Where are we?" Lauren asked, glancing around.

Stefan looked pleased. "This is my home, Mrs. Trent," he said with a smile. "Come. I will introduce you to my Ana. Then I must get back to Brno and meet Jordan when he arrives."

"Does he know where you live?"

"No. Both Jordan and I have become domesticated since last we worked together. It is good that our wives get this opportunity to meet."

Lauren saw no point in trying to explain the situation. Since Jordan had introduced her as his wife, she supposed she shouldn't say anything to cause anyone to doubt him.

When Stefan came around the car and lifted her out, Lauren became aware of how she was dressed. The thin cotton gown fell to her knees in a nondescript fashion. And she was barefoot! How would Stefan ever explain this to his wife?

She needn't have worried. The young woman who met them at the door was filled with concern and bustled around making Lauren feel welcomed and comfortable.

Stefan explained that Ana would need to find Lauren something to wear and that he would be back as soon as he could return with her husband.

Both the women nodded and he left.

As soon as Ana discovered that Lauren could speak her language she happily chattered to her, showing her skirts and blouses and having her try on shoes. Within a very short while Lauren felt as though she'd made a friend.

By the time Stefan found Jordan, Jordan had spent several lifetimes, at least he was sure it had been that long, looking for Stefan.

"Where have you been!" he demanded as soon as Stefan appeared.

Jordan had ended up going back to the curio shop and waiting in the back room, knowing that sooner or later Stefan would come looking for him.

"Getting your wife to safety," he said mildly.

Jordan sat down suddenly and just looked at his friend for a moment. "Is she okay?"

"She's fine."

"Did they recognize her?"

"No, although we cut it a little close, my friend. They were planning to move her this morning."

"Where?" Jordan asked, getting to his feet with renewed energy.

Stefan relayed the information Lauren had passed on to him during their drive.

"That's the best lead we've gotten as to who's behind all of this." He looked around the room. "Can you take me to her?"

Stefan laughed. "I was only waiting for you to ask. After all, maybe you grow tired of this wife of yours, huh? Could be you aren't so very anxious to see her again?"

"Very funny, Stefan. Let's go," he said, starting for the door.

"No. Not together. You must go back to the park and wait for me there." He described the car he was driving. "I will pick you up once I am sure no one is watching you."

"Of course you're right. I'm getting careless."

"No. You are a man in love. I recognize the symptoms, since I suffer from them myself."

"You? What are you talking about?"

"I left your very beautiful wife with my lovely wife, Ana. They will be telling each other all of our secrets if we do not get back there soon, eh?" He clapped Jordan on the back. "Now go. I will find you."

Jordan went over to the park, realizing that he hadn't eaten for the past twenty-four hours. Now that he knew Lauren was safe, he had relaxed enough to notice.

He never wanted to go through anything like these past few hours again. He couldn't remember ever having been quite so apprehensive about anything before.

Whenever he'd been in a dangerous situation, he'd known that he would do his best to get himself out of it. And if his best wasn't good enough, only he would suffer the consequences.

This assignment had been different. He'd never before felt such a strong sense of responsibility. If anything had happened to Lauren— Yes, Jordan? an inner voice asked. What then? The pain that shot through him must have had something to do with hunger. He'd known other operatives who hadn't come back from assignments. And Lauren had known what she was getting into, hadn't she?

And if you'd lost her? What then?

Jordan faced the fact that nothing in his life would ever have been the same.

Lauren was special. She was his. She had given herself to him, a beautiful giving, just as he had given himself to her. He was no longer a loner, needing no one. For the first time since he'd lost his mother, Jordan admitted that he needed someone—a very special someone.

He saw Stefan's car approaching. He started walking as though to cross the street. At the last moment, he swerved and crawled into the car.

"Well?" he asked.

"No tails that I can see."

"How about you?"

"Who, me?" Stefan asked with an innocent grin. "Now who would want to watch me?"

"Probably every official in the country, if they had any sense."

"Ah, but there you have it, my friend. They find me a pitiful specimen and not worth the time it would take to keep an eye on me."

"Hah. Little do they know."

They smiled at each other and rode along in silence. By the time Stefan turned onto the road out of town Jordan was asleep.

Lauren heard the car drive up and peered through the window. It was Stefan and he had someone with him! Eagerly she ran to the door and threw it open, only to come to a stumbling halt. The man who got out of the car was unshaven and his clothes looked as though he'd worn them for weeks without cleaning them. The dilapidated cap pulled down low over his eyes made him look as if he made his living mugging unsuspecting passersby in dark alleyways.

Then Stefan said something and laughed, pointing to Lauren.

The man with him looked up and grinned. Lauren would recognize that smile anywhere, in any disguise.

"Jordan!" she cried joyously and ran toward him.

He met her halfway, grabbing her and holding her close. God, she felt so good, right there in his arms where she belonged.

"You okay?" he asked in a gruff voice.

"Of course I'm okay. You never doubted that, did you?" she asked, looking up at him, her arms around his neck.

He'd never seen that look on her face before. There was no worry or strain, just sheer happiness radiating from her. Because of him? Jordan felt humbled by the thought. Was it possible that he was that important to her?

"Oh, Lauren," he muttered, then pulled her to him in a searing kiss.

He didn't know how long they stood there in front of the small cottage. He never wanted to let her go. Stefan finally came up and clapped him on the back. "Come inside, my friend. Perhaps you would like something to eat. For myself, I'm starved."

Jordan reluctantly removed his arms from around her and they walked into the house together.

Stefan proudly introduced Ana and then Ana and Lauren pointed out the choice of clothes Lauren had made and the men agreed she would do very well as Jordan's wife dressed as she was.

"When are we leaving?" Lauren asked a little later, after they had finished eating. She looked at first one man, then the other.

Stefan looked at the deep lines of weariness in his friend's face and answered for him. "I think you will both be safe to stay here tonight. I will help you get to the border tomorrow."

"But Franz told me to be back tonight."

"What's one more night, my friend? Franz is an old woman, always worrying about everything. He enjoys being in control. It makes him feel very important."

Now that he had finally stopped long enough to eat and relax, Jordan felt as though he could go to sleep sitting in the chair.

"You're probably right, Stefan. Anyway, I'm so tired, I'm punchy. If you don't mind, we'll stay here and head back tomorrow."

Ana hopped up, saying, "I have already prepared the guest room, just in case you would stay. Come, Lauren, I will find you a gown to sleep in."

Lauren gazed uncertainly at Jordan. Wasn't he going to tell them the truth? He glanced up and saw her worried expression, not understanding its cause. "What's wrong?" he asked. "Don't you want to stay?"

"It's not that—" she began, her face flushing, and Jordan suddenly remembered. He'd gotten so used to thinking of her as his wife that he'd actually forgotten it was all part of the charade.

As far as that went, there was no reason to make any explanations at this point. He smiled at her reassuringly. "I promise not to pull covers," he said with a grin. "And I'll do my best to keep you warm."

Stefan's laugh made her cheeks turn even rosier and Lauren turned away to follow Ana into the other room.

"Lauren?" Jordan said softly.

She turned around and looked at him.

"I'm only teasing you."

"I know."

"You probably won't even know I'm there. I'm so tired I'm not sure I'll be able to stumble to the bedroom."

She smiled, then glanced at Stefan. "Sounds like a tremendous number of excuses, doesn't it? Do you suppose he's trying to get out of performing his husbandly duties?"

Stefan nodded emphatically. "That it does, Lauren. That it does."

Jordan slowly stood and stretched, his arms high over his head. With a slow wink at Stefan, he said, "I said I was tired, Lauren, not dead," and began to stalk her with a deliberate tread.

Nine

Lauren turned and fled down the hallway, the sound of the men's laughter ringing in her ears. She almost ran into Ana who was coming out of her bedroom.

"Oh, I'm sorry," Ana said.

"It wasn't your fault. I was trying to get away from their teasing."

"Oh, that Stefan. He enjoys making jokes."

"Yes, so does Jordan. No wonder they are such good friends."

"I am very glad to be able to meet Jordan Trent. Stefan speaks of him often. He says that once Jordan saved his life. He will never forget that. Ever."

"Yes, I know that feeling."

Ana looked down at the garment she was holding and thrust it out to Lauren. "Here. This should be warm enough for you tonight."

Remembering Jordan's comment about keeping her warm, Lauren refused to meet Ana's eyes. "Thank you." She took the nightgown and then on impulse hugged the other woman. "You've been so kind," she said, tears filling her eyes.

Ana patted her cheek. "You are a very easy person to be kind to, Lauren. I am so glad we were able to meet."

"So am I."

Lauren smiled at the other woman, then went into the bedroom across the hallway.

Lauren had carefully folded the borrowed clothes that she would have to wear tomorrow and was reaching for the borrowed gown when the door behind her opened and she heard Jordan say, "You don't have to wear that on my account, you know."

Out of a lifelong habit of modesty, Lauren held the gown up to her and turned around to face him.

He'd obviously showered and shaved, and was wearing only the pants he'd had on earlier.

"I'm so glad you made it all right," she said, her heart overflowing with gratitude to be with him once again.

He slowly walked over to her and gently removed the gown from her hands. "I'm so glad that you're glad. I wouldn't have blamed you if you'd wished all sorts of ills on me."

"Don't say that, Jordan. You've never done anything that I haven't wanted you to do."

He lightly drew a line from her chin, down her throat and between her breasts. "Even now?"

"Especially now," she said with a small smile.

"You're insatiable, woman," he said with a pleased grin.

"And you're exhausted," she said with an understanding look. The dark shadows under his eyes were more noticeable now that she was closer to him.

"Never that exhausted, love," he whispered, picking her up and placing her on the bed. Then he reached over and turned out the light.

They were wakened early the next morning by Stefan's pounding on their door. "All right, you two. If you intend to catch a ride into Brno with me, you'd better hurry. I'm leaving in ten minutes."

Lauren sat up, horrified to discover that they had both overslept. She glanced at Jordan. He hadn't moved from his position on his stomach, his pillow half-covering his head.

"Jordan?"

"Mmmmph?"

"Did you hear Stefan? He said—"

With his head still under the pillow Jordan muttered, "Of course I heard Stefan. How could anyone possibly sleep through that?"

"Oh. Well, you didn't move and I thought—"

"I didn't move because I'm convinced my body will shatter into a dozen pieces if I dare wiggle even a toe."

She leaned over him with a worried expression. "Oh, Jordan, what's wrong? Did you get hurt? Last night you seemed to be—"

"Last night I must have thought I was some damned teenager, showing off," he muttered, then groaned as he slowly rolled over.

She quickly stifled a giggle when she realized he was all right.

And he was certainly all right, having proven that quite satisfactorily on more than one occasion the night before. Making love in the privacy of a bedroom with thick walls had been a new and enjoyable experience for her. Lauren had a hunch that making love with Jordan at any time, anywhere, and under most any condition she could think of would be a new and enjoyable experience for her.

"We need to get up."

"I know," he said, continuing to lie on his back with his arms outspread and his eyes closed. The dark shadows were gone from beneath his eyes and the lines of strain had disappeared as well. Amazing what a good night's rest would do for a person, she decided with a smile.

Lauren's education had been extensively broadened the night before. One of the things she had learned was a certain area along Jordan's abdomen where he was quite ticklish. Accidently discovered, the small but vital area now gave Lauren a certain feeling of power over the man lying so relaxed beside her.

Testing her new theory she leaned over and very lightly touched his lower abdomen with her tongue. In an astonishingly short time Jordan was on his feet staring at her in indignation. "That's not fair and you know it!"

She climbed out of bed and quickly began to put on the clothes she'd tidily folded the night before. "We can't miss our ride, can we, Jordan?" she asked with her brows slightly arched.

He stalked around the bed and grabbed her. "I happen to know some rather ticklish places on you, too, you know," he said ominously.

She nodded. "I know."

"But I would never stoop so low as to take advantage of such intimate knowledge."

"Me, either."

"Like hell."

Her saucy smile was too endearing to ignore. He laughed and grabbed her to him. Giving her a hearty kiss, he said, "Just wait. I'll get even."

She slipped her shoes on and opened the door enough to get out. Then she stuck her head back in and said, "I can hardly wait."

Stefan waited with good-natured impatience while they quickly drank some coffee and buttered some breakfast rolls to take with them. Then they were on their way.

The men sat up front and discussed the best way to get back to the border from Brno. Lauren listened with half a mind. The day was so beautiful. It was hard to imagine that anything bad would happen anywhere at any time on such a day as this.

She was in love and all was right with her world. Lauren studied the back of Jordan's head while he, unaware of her gaze, talked with Stefan. She loved the shape of his ears and the way his hair curled along the nape of his neck. How could she ever have thought this man looked harsh and intimidating?

Well, perhaps he was intimidating. But not to her. Never to her. She loved to watch his expression change whenever he caught sight of her. She'd never seen him look at anyone else that way. She wondered if he was aware of how differently he treated her.

Was it their lovemaking that had changed him? Did all men automatically treat a woman they'd gone to bed with differently? She wished she knew more about men, and more about how they thought. It wasn't something she'd feel comfortable discussing with her father.

There was a possibility that Jordan was falling in love with her, though, wasn't there? His tenderness toward her, his protectiveness, his gentleness, his inability to be near her without reaching out to touch her cheek. All of those things must mean that he considered her someone special in his life.

But did it mean that she would see him again once they returned to the States? Even working for the same agency they'd never had any reason to come into contact before. Of course now they knew each other. Maybe when he was in the office he'd stop in to see her, maybe ask her out to dinner, and then— Then what, silly? What are all these daydreams about, anyway? she thought impatiently. Do you think this man would really change his entire way of life in order to make you a part of it?

I can dream, can't I?

Of course you can dream, as long as you don't get your dreams confused with reality.

In that case, she would create her own reality. Lauren closed her eyes and began to picture a little girl with reddish-blond hair and big brown eyes, and an infant boy with black curly hair and gray eyes.

By the time they reached the outskirts of Brno the men had decided that Jordan and Lauren should wait until midafternoon to head for the border. They wouldn't be able to cross until late that night anyway, and they had better opportunities for concealment there in Brno.

In the meantime Stefan would try to find out what had happened at the clinic once it had been discovered that Lauren was gone.

The day seemed to creep by while they waited in a warehouse in the manufacturing district. They'd arranged a ride with another truck driver who knew Stefan and agreed that he could use the extra cash for his family.

Jordan didn't want to take any chances on being seen by someone who might have noticed them earlier in their roles as tourists, so they waited in the privacy of the warehouse.

Lauren discovered that Jordan was no longer as reticent about his early life as he'd been at first. He seemed willing enough to answer her questions and seemed to gain some amount of relief in sharing the trauma of losing his mother and being thrust into an entirely different environment.

She, in turn, shared much of her early, more happy, childhood with him, even to telling the story of how her parents met.

"You'd like my parents, I think," she said at one point.

"Ah, but would they like me, that is the question."

"Why wouldn't they like you?" she demanded, the light of fanaticism shining in her eyes.

He grinned at her vehemence. "Oh, I don't know. There's something about trying to explain how I make my living."

"You're a sales rep from Chicago," she promptly retorted.

"Is that what you'd tell them?" he asked, surprised.

"Of course. That's what you tell everyone, isn't it?"

"Well, yes."

"Isn't that what your father thinks you do?"

"Yes."

"Well, then," she said, as though the matter were settled.

Perhaps it was.

The trucker showed up with sandwiches for them, and the news that he needed to leave in order to get back home at a decent hour.

Since they were definitely traveling light, Jordan and Lauren had no trouble getting ready to leave. She glanced back at the cavernous building with affection. This was the place where Jordan had shared some of his most intimate feelings. She had a hunch he'd never done that before, with anyone.

It was almost like discovering that the man she loved was a virgin. He'd saved his most intimate thoughts and emotions for her. She smiled at the whimsical thought.

It was dark by the time they reached the turnoff to Franz's hut. Jordan paid the driver and they stood watching the man as he turned around and went back the way they had come.

"Where to now?" she asked, looking around.

"The first of many long walks, I'm afraid. I hope you're up to it."

"Don't worry about me. I'm fine."

"Glad to hear it. Now I can devote my energies to more weighty concerns."

She grinned at him, pleased that he was in such a good mood.

Later she was glad Jordan was in a good mood because Franz certainly wasn't.

"I waited up all night for you. Didn't I tell you that you must be back last night?"

"Yes, you mentioned it," Jordan said politely. "And I tried, but it was impossible. So here we are."

"Yes. And what am I supposed to do with you, just tell me that?"

"Help us across the border."

"Yes. That would have been an easy enough task last night because the guard that substitutes at the crossing on Wednesday night has learned to look the other way when there are those who wish to travel quickly between the two countries."

"I see," Jordan said slowly.

"It will be another week before he will be substituting for the other man's night off."

"We can't wait that long."

"Of course you can't. It would be too dangerous for all of us."

"We'll just have to take our chances."

"And get yourselves killed."

"Believe me, I intend to avoid that possibility with every ounce of energy I have."

Franz shook his head and got up from the table.
"Crazy Americans and their women," he muttered in
a foreboding voice, walking over to the stove.

"What are we going to do?" Lauren asked Jordan
in a low voice.

"I'm inclined to agree with Stefan about Franz. He
enjoys being the voice of doom. The border along here
is sketchily covered because there are no towns on
either side for many miles. One guard has to patrol
long stretches. We'll just watch and wait for our
chance."

She nodded. The sooner they left this unpleasant
man's house, the better. He had barely spoken to her,
ignoring her as though she were some pet Jordan had
brought in with him, one whom Franz wasn't sure he
wanted in his house!

They waited a couple of hours and then followed
Franz into the woods behind his hut. Lauren was glad
he seemed to know where he was going. There seemed
to be no trail to follow and the undergrowth was thick
and, at some points, impenetrable.

They seemed to have walked for miles when Franz
raised his hand, motioning for them to keep silent.
Since no one had said anything for hours, Lauren
thought he was being unnecessarily dramatic.

With sign language he pointed out the sentry out-
post, the barbed wire that ran in parallel strips a few
hundred yards apart. In the moonlight, the strip of
ground between the wires appeared to be a barren, no-
man's-land. There were no trees or shrubs to use as
cover. They would be totally exposed from the time
they left the wooded area where they now stood until

they managed to get through both sets of heavily wired fences. The woods began on the far side of the second fence.

Lauren watched as Jordan signed back. The two men shook hands and Franz walked away in the direction he had come.

Jordan came over and knelt down beside her where she rested against a tree. "Okay, love, we're on our own now and—"

He'd just lost her attention to anything he might have to say after the unaccustomed endearment. Then she forced herself to concentrate on his low-voiced instructions.

"I want you to try to get as much rest as you can. I'm going to watch and try to figure out the pattern this sentry uses. Once I figure out his routine, we'll slip past him as soon as he returns to the other side. You understand?"

She nodded.

Jordan gazed into her eyes and felt as though he were drowning in their depths. The darkness in the woods could not eliminate the glow in her eyes. He ran his hand along the nape of her neck and massaged her tense neck and shoulder muscles for a few minutes. Her sigh was almost soundless.

He leaned over and kissed her softly. "Get some sleep. We've got a long hike still ahead of us. But at least it will be in Austrian countryside."

Lauren thought it would be impossible to fall asleep in the middle of the woods, but she stretched out on the soft needles and the next thing she knew Jordan was shaking her shoulder, his hand lightly covering her mouth. When she opened her eyes he lifted his hand. Leaning over, he whispered in her ear, "We're going to cross in another few minutes. He's due down here any time. As soon as he turns away we're going to cross."

"But what if he decides to turn around?"

"Pray that he doesn't, that's all. We need all the time we can get before he turns to face this section again. Okay?"

She nodded her head. It had to be okay. They had no choice.

Lauren watched as the guard came toward them. The moonlight was so bright that he seemed to be in a spotlight as he moved along. The contrast between the moonlight and the shadows from the woods gave them excellent cover. They waited while he walked past them for several hundred yards.

He turned and slowly began his trek back toward the sentry box. He'd seemed to be only a few short yards away when Jordan breathed into her ear the word, "Now!"

Taking her hand he began to run. Lauren had never moved so fast in her life. She didn't think her feet ever touched the ground. Then he was pushing her down to the ground while he rapidly worked wire cutters along the bottom of the fence.

He helped her wiggle through, then followed her. He took her hand once more as they raced across the brightly lit area between the fences. Lauren kept waiting to hear a yell but everything was eerily still in the moonlight. The landscape seemed unreal; it was as though they were surrounded by a backdrop for some theatrical performance.

Once again they followed the previous procedure: she lay still while he used the wire cutters.

Then all hell broke loose. There was a shout, then more shouts. Dogs began to bark, a siren went off and searchlights pinned them to the ground.

"What the hell!" Jordan exclaimed, still working frantically. Lifting the fence he shoved her under, yelling "Run! Get to the shelter of the trees. I'm right behind you."

She did what she was told. Lauren was almost to the safety of the trees when she heard the ominous sound of automatic weapons being fired. She spun around and saw Jordan racing toward her, yelling for her to keep going. Then, as though in slow motion, she saw him stumble and slowly spin before falling limply to the ground.

He didn't move.

Ten

Lauren screamed, "Jordan!" and, oblivious to the steady staccato of gunfire, ran back to him. "Jordan!" she cried again, frantically wiping the tears from her eyes so that she could see him.

The searchlights went off and the sirens were stopped mid-blast, leaving a deafening silence in their place. Lauren looked around and realized that they had made it. They were in Austria. But Jordan—

She had to see where he'd been hit. She had to get him to a hospital. He was hurt but he was going to be all right. He had to be all right.

He lay on his side, his head shadowed. She felt along his back and her hand came away wet and sticky. "Oh, Jordan," she sobbed.

Jordan groaned, the sweetest sound she'd ever heard.

"Jordan?"

"Run, Lauren, you've got to run," he muttered.

"Oh, darling. We don't have to run. We made it. We're safe. Oh, God, please let him be all right," she whispered.

"Leave me, Lauren. Find a house and explain, someone will take you in."

"You're damn right they will, but I'm not leaving you, Jordan Trent. You're coming with me if I have to carry you every foot of the way."

"Funny," he murmured, "never heard you curse before."

"I never had a good enough reason to before." She got up on her knees. "Help me, darling, please. Please try to stand."

She didn't know how long it took her to get him to his feet. Lauren was so afraid that he was going to black out on her. Then what would she do?

She wouldn't think about it.

Slowly she began to edge him through the woods, wondering where to go and how long he could keep moving. It took all of her strength to hold him upright.

"Don't do this to yourself, Lauren," he managed to say. "I'll make it. I'm too tough to quit now."

"You'd better be, you arrogant macho male. I want you to show me what you've got. Show me that indomitable will, that refusal to give up. I dare you!" Tears still streamed down her face and she forced herself to continue forward, one slow step at a time, guiding him.

When she first saw the light shining through the trees, she thought she was imagining it. Would a house be this close to the border? Then she realized it was moving.

"Help!" she hollered. "Please, will you help us?"

The answering shout was the most welcome thing she had ever heard. Three men approached them warily.

"My husband's been shot. We're Americans. Can you help get him to the hospital?"

Her words, spoken in German, seemed to galvanize them into action. Two of the men stepped forward just in time to catch Jordan as he toppled over.

Jordan kept having the craziest dreams. He and Lauren were on the beach of Santiago Island in the South Seas. The warm breeze felt so good against his hot skin. Every once in a while he and Lauren would run out into the water of the lagoon that was protected from the heavy ocean waves by a coral reef near the point.

The cool water took away the feeling of heat and he would surface in time to see Lauren's eyes, her beautiful, misty-gray eyes, looking at him with a worried expression.

"Your eyes are so beautiful," he whispered, only to discover that his mouth was so dry he could barely speak.

"Hush, darling, don't waste your energy talking," Lauren said anxiously.

"I'm so thirsty," he tried to say, but somehow his mouth wouldn't work right.

Lauren seemed to know because she slipped a couple of slivers of ice in his mouth.

"The water feels great, doesn't it?" he asked.

"Whatever you say. Please try to rest. You're going to be fine."

Of course he was going to be fine. Why shouldn't he be fine? He had a lovely wife and two adorable children. Or did he? Of course he did. "Matthew Mackenzie Trent," Jordan stated in a clear, concise voice.

Oh dear Lord, please let him be all right. He's hallucinating or something. Let his mind be all right. He's running such a terribly high fever. Please take care of him for me.

Jordan seemed to relax and fall back into a restless sleep and Lauren sat back down in the chair where she'd kept a vigil for the past three days.

They were at an American base somewhere in Germany. She had called Mallory and he'd set some powerful wheels in motion. Within hours after Jordan's arrival at the local hospital, Mallory himself had arrived and supervised Jordan's transfer.

They'd had to operate to remove the bullet lodged in his back. The doctor said it was a miracle that it had missed so many vital organs as well as the spinal column.

Mallory had already heard from Frances and Trevor Monroe and was quite pleased with the way Jordan had handled everything.

"He's going to make it, you know," Mallory had assured her that morning. "That man's too damned stubborn to die."

"I know," she said.

"Are you ready to go home?"

"You mean now?"

"I mean whenever you're ready. Your assignment has been officially terminated. You did an outstanding job, Lauren."

"Thank you, sir."

"Now, about going home—"

"What about Jordan?"

"What about him?"

"When will he be able to go home?"

"The surgeon hasn't said."

"Then if it's all right with you, sir, I'll wait until we can go home at the same time." She struggled to try to find the right words. "You see, we started this together. I think we should finish it together."

"I see," Mallory said thoughtfully. "That's very professional of you, looking at it like that. From the way he behaved in the beginning, I somehow had the feeling you would be eager to get away from him."

"Oh, no, sir. Jordan and I became friends."

"Friends, huh?" Mallory studied her for a few minutes in silence. "A man can't have too many friends, can he?"

She smiled. "I think we'll be able to return home no later than next week, sir. If that's all right."

"I suppose it will have to be," he said drily.

Now Lauren studied the sleeping man who lay so quietly. She'd already discovered that whenever he became restless she could calm him by talking to him.

Tonight had been the first time he'd done much talking. Unfortunately it hadn't made much sense.

Why had he said Matthew Mackenzie Trent with such obvious pride? Did he somehow think they were back in Brno, making silly conversation to entertain whoever might be listening to them?

"Run, Lauren! For God's sake, run!"

His sudden shout startled her and she quickly stood up. The floor nurses must have heard him as well. They came racing into the room.

"I think he's reliving the time he was shot," she whispered to them. Meanwhile she continued to stroke his hand, something she'd found calmed him.

"As long as we're here, I think we should check his bandages." As gently as possible they rolled him onto his side and checked for seepage.

"He's healing nicely," the nurse in charge said with a smile. "I know you must be relieved, Mrs. Trent."

"Oh! I'm—I, uh—Yes, I'm extremely pleased," she finally managed to say.

However, it was another week before the surgeon arranged to have him flown by military transport back to the States. Lauren wasn't exactly sure what strings Mallory pulled, but he arranged for her to fly back with Jordan.

"Where are we?" Jordan asked in a faint voice.

"Walter Reed Hospital," Lauren said with a smile.

"How did I get here?"

"You were flown in from Germany."

"Germany? We were supposed to be in Austria."

She smiled at the querulous tone of his voice. That told her, like nothing else, that he was beginning to feel better.

"We were in Austria. Then you were flown to Germany, where they took a bullet out of your back; then you were flown here."

"Oh." He was quiet for several minutes. Finally he asked, "What are you doing here?"

"Protecting the nurses from you," she said with a grin.

"What's that supposed to mean?"

"That you can be a real pain at times."

"Tell me something I don't know."

She studied him for a moment in silence, then softly said, "You can be a real love at times."

"Oh, yeah? Says who?"

"Says me."

"So what do you know?"

"I know that I'm very glad to see you feeling better."

He squeezed her hand. "I'm glad to be feeling better, too. I was getting a little tired of fading in and out. Although some of my dreams were pretty nice, at that."

"Hmmm. What kind of dreams, or should I ask?"

"Well, since you were in them, I suppose you have a certain right to know."

She could feel the heat in her cheeks at his teasing.

"You and I were on Santiago Island together."

"Where's that?"

"That's the island where I was trying to take a long overdue vacation when Mallory insisted I had to come back to work."

"As soon as you're feeling better, I'm sure you can go back."

"I just might do that. Catch up on my fishing, my reading, my sleep." He interrupted his list. "That's a laugh, isn't it? That's all I've done is sleep lately. They keep me so doped up."

"Helps your body heal faster when you're relaxed."

"Lauren?"

"Hmmm?"

"I never thanked you for saving my life."

"Don't be silly. I didn't save you from anything."

"I distinctly remember a lecture about my arrogant, macho attitude."

"You remember my saying that?"

"It rang in my ears for days afterwards."

"I was scared. I thought you were going to die."

"So did I." His voice showed no sign of amusement.

"Thank you for risking your life by coming back in to get me," she said.

"That was part of my job."

"Oh."

"I couldn't have just left you over there, you know."

"I guess not."

Jordan took her hand and laced his fingers through it. "You are one very special lady, you know that, don't you?"

"Not really."

"I will never forget you," he said softly.

But you intend to try, Lauren realized with a certainty that flashed the words across her mind.

Fighting to keep her composure she said, "I will never forget you, either."

"I'm sure you won't. I'll always remind you of the worst nightmare of your life."

"No," she said, shaking her head.

He smiled. "I can't imagine why you've been hanging around this hospital so much. Every time I wake up, you're here."

And you don't want me here, but don't want to hurt my feelings by asking me to leave.

"I was just making sure you were doing all right, that's all. Actually, Mr. Mallory expects me to come back to work as soon as possible."

"He would," Jordan muttered.

Lauren knew that if she didn't get out of there she would burst into tears. What had she expected, his undying gratitude? A proposal of marriage, for heaven's sake? "Can I bring you anything?" she asked brightly.

Jordan studied her face, her wonderful, dear face. How had he ever managed without her in his life? He could hardly wait until he was on his feet so that he could tell her. There was so much he had to say; they had so many plans to make.

After all, he wasn't getting any younger. They needed to get started on that family they talked about. He smiled at the thought.

"I can't think of anything right now, but thanks," he said, wishing he was strong enough to hold her and kiss her. Damn! He was as weak as a three-day-old kitten, and just about as useless.

"Well, then if you don't mind, I think I'll go." She pointed to the buzzer that was pinned to the bed. "If you want the nurse, you just touch that button."

"Fine. Thanks." He watched as she began to edge toward the door.

"Lauren?"

"Yes?"

"Don't I even get a farewell kiss?"

She closed her eyes for two heartbeats, then forced them open. "Of course." Walking over to him, she leaned down and pressed her lips softly against his.

She smelled so fresh, like springtime. He touched the curl in front of her ear. "I'll see you later," he said.

She nodded, unable to say another word.

He watched her walk out of the room, then began his impatient wait for her to return.

She never did.

Eleven

Jordan strode down the hallway toward Mallory's office and noticed that, once again, staff members were scattering before him. He shook his head. Some things changed; other things always seemed to remain the same.

He opened the door to Mallory's office and strode in. Mallory was on the phone.

Jordan sat down a little carefully. The doctor had been furious with him for insisting on leaving. But he'd been in that damned hospital for three weeks. What the hell did they expect?

Mallory lifted a brow at him to acknowledge his presence, but otherwise ignored Jordan. Jordan wished he could wave a magic wand and make Mallory himself disappear. Looking around the room, Jordan realized that nothing had changed since the day two months ago when he'd walked in there and had his life turned upside down, inside out and scattered all over the floor.

He didn't seem to know how to put all the pieces together because one very vital piece was missing. Lauren.

Mallory hung up the phone and asked, "What are you doing out of the hospital?"

"I got sick of the nurses."

"No worse than they were sick of you, believe me. I understand they were having to give combat pay to the nurses who were assigned to your room."

"Very funny. Now where is she?"

Mallory glanced around the room as though expecting someone to suddenly materialize.

"Who?"

"Don't give me that, Mallory. What have you done with Lauren Mackenzie?"

Mallory leaned back in his chair and placed his feet on his desk. Then he took his time lighting a cigarette. "She has taken a leave of absence."

"Damn it, Mallory," Jordan said leaning forward, then suddenly wincing. "I know she's taken a leave of absence, even though I had to get out of the hospital and do some sleuthing to discover that information. She has also sublet her apartment. So where is she?"

Mallory studied the other man, noticing the pallor in his face and the strain in his expression. The recent ordeal had certainly taken its toll. There was a fine tremor in Jordan's hands, but none in his voice. Of course he'd had a great deal of practice exercising his voice by barking at the nurses.

"Maybe she went back to Pennsylvania."

"Maybe? Don't you know?"

"I don't generally keep tabs on all the employees in this building, J.D."

"Since when? You seem to know every move I make, sometimes before I make it. Are you finally admitting your mental telepathy abilities have failed?"

"Why do you want to find Lauren? Everything wrapped up nicely in that deal."

"Because we have some unfinished business to take care of."

Mallory made a steeple of his fingers and rested his chin on them. "I wasn't aware of any unfinished business."

"Will wonders never cease? The man is a mere mortal after all."

"What unfinished business?"

"It isn't really any of your concern, Mallory, but when has that ever stopped you?" Jordan stood with slow, precise movements and wandered over to the window. Summer had arrived while he wasn't looking. Several things had happened while he wasn't looking, as a matter of fact; one of them being that he'd lost his heart. "I need to find Lauren so that we can get married."

"Aaahhh," Mallory said using a tone of enlightenment. "So Lauren has agreed to marry you."

"I didn't say that. But she will, if I can just find her."

Mallory didn't bother hiding his smile since Jordan's back was to him. "You've never lacked confidence, I'll give you that," he said.

"That's what you think."

"So. You and Lauren are getting married. How is that going to affect your job?"

Jordan glanced over his shoulder. "How do you think?"

"I think it's time you learned how the world looks from behind this desk," Mallory said quietly.

That drew Jordan back toward the other man. "What are you talking about?"

"I've been waiting for the right time to turn this job over to you. You've got the best, or at least the most devious, mind around. With you plotting covert activities, our respected enemies will never know what to expect next."

"You're serious."

"Never more serious in my life."

Jordan glanced around the room again. "What do you intend to do?"

"Oh, I won't be far. They're pushing me upstairs, with a big thanks to you and the way you handled that last matter. You made everyone in the department look good."

"We had some lucky breaks—the biggest ones being that no one recognized Mrs. Monroe or noticed the switch before we had a chance to get Lauren out of there."

"Has anyone told you what was behind the kidnapping?"

"No."

"A group of would-be saviors of mankind had decided to force some changes on the western world. Frances Monroe was only the first of many such planned hostages. They were preparing a similar kidnapping in Moscow."

"Moscow! You mean a Communist captive?"

"Yep. As a matter of fact, they were close to grabbing the Premier's wife."

"My God! They were out of their minds."

"What they're trying to do is to stop world war. They just had a rather bizarre way of going about it."

Jordan shook his head. Then he began to think of what he would do, or not do, if someone was holding Lauren as prisoner. The way he felt about her, he would do whatever he had to do to keep her safe and...

Maybe their idea wasn't so crazy after all. But he was glad he'd been able to stop it from going any farther.

"You changed the subject, Mallory. I want to know where she is."

"Employees' records are confidential, J.D. You know that."

Jordan repeated a colorful display of obscenities for Mallory, concluding with exactly what he could do with his confidentiality.

"Why would any woman in her right mind want to marry you, J.D.?" he asked, shaking his head ruefully.

Mallory had just verbalized the question that had haunted Jordan for weeks, ever since he realized that Lauren wasn't coming back to the hospital.

What had he ever done to show her how he felt about her? That she was the most important person in the world to him? That he wasn't really sure how he would manage if she wasn't a part of his life?

The thought of never seeing Lauren again frightened him like nothing else had in his life.

"I want the opportunity to discuss the matter with her," he finally said.

Mallory shrugged, then reached into his top desk drawer and took out a pad of paper. Ripping off the top sheet, he handed it to Jordan.

"You had that all the time!" Jordan said, his voice rising. "And you intended to give it to me all along!"

"Actually, I'd been waiting for you to ask for it politely; perhaps add a please, maybe a thank you." He put his cigarette out in an overflowing ashtray. "Unfortunately being in love didn't help your disposition any more than your vacation did."

Jordan studied the older man for a moment in silence. "When did you know?" he asked.

"By the time you walked out of this office the day you met her."

"You're crazy. I didn't even like her."

"There was too much friction and smoke not to burst into flame sooner or later. It was only a matter of time."

He looked at his boss with suspicion. "Did you set me up?"

"Who, me? Hell, no. I just needed someone to put at this desk and knew you'd have to really want to give up fieldwork in order to consider it."

"So Lauren was to help sweeten the pie?"

Mallory allowed himself a small smile. "Do I look like a matchmaker?"

"You look like the most devious man I've ever known. Funny you should admire that trait in me."

"It takes one to know one, I suppose." He drew his feet off the desk and stood up. Nodding toward the slip of paper Mallory said, "You got what you came for, so why don't you get out of here and let me get some work done."

Jordan folded the paper as though it were a map to priceless treasure. As far as he was concerned, it was. He was already out the door when he heard Mallory call his name. Jordan stuck his head back in.

"Yes?"

"You've got two months vacation waiting for you, and the Santiago Island police have discovered they merely misunderstood my earlier message. You are wanted by the government because you're extremely valuable to us. I'm sure you will find that they'll treat you with utmost respect and awe if you should decide to return."

Jordan grinned. "Thanks."

Mallory reached for his pack of cigarettes. "The least I could do," he muttered.

Jordan closed the door and went whistling down the hallway. Several people stopped and stared. They had never seen Jordan Trent in such a good mood.

Jordan spotted the street sign up ahead with a sense of satisfaction. The sign reflected the same name as the one scribbled on the paper he'd been carefully guarding. He turned at the corner. The homes had been built during another era. They were set back from the street with shade trees dotting expansive lawns. Most of the homes had inviting porches built in front, with chairs and porch swings waiting to be enjoyed.

This was the street where Lauren had been brought up. It could have been the back lot of Universal Studios. He expected to see James Stewart come walking out of one of the houses any minute, waving goodbye to Donna Reed and patting a golden retriever on the head.

Jordan could almost feel the friendliness of the people, something that was lacking in the neighborhood where he'd been brought up in Chicago. Watching the house numbers, he spotted hers three houses away.

His heart was pounding so hard in his chest that he was having trouble breathing. He could feel a cold sweat pop out on his forehead. This was ridiculous. He kept more calm when he was working than he was now.

Jordan had just realized, now that he'd found Lauren, that he didn't know what to say. What if she didn't want to see him? What if she had actually been hiding from him? Why else had she requested a leave of absence?

What was he doing in Reading, Pennsylvania?

The answer to that was simple: being a coward. *Where's all that damn courage you rely on so heavily?* he demanded to know, but got no answer.

Pulling up in front of the house, he stared at it intently. There were two stories and a dormer window that indicated a good-size attic. Cheerfully painted shutters decorated the windows. Roses bloomed along the front walk. Any minute he expected to see Judy

Garland dance out onto the front porch singing "Meet Me in St. Louis."

He was cracking up. The strain of the past several weeks had been too much for him. Forcing himself to remove the keys from the ignition, Jordan slowly climbed out of the car and began the long walk toward the house.

The garage was in back. He had no idea if anyone was at home or not. By this time he wasn't sure that he cared. Maybe this wasn't the best way to handle things. A phone call might be more practical—maybe set up a time when they could meet. He ignored his cravenness and continued the long walk.

Until now, he'd been able to live with the hope of convincing Lauren that she would do well to marry him. Soon he would have to face the reality of what she thought of the idea.

He wasn't at all sure he could deal with that reality.

Stepping up on the porch, he walked over to the door and rang the doorbell. The wooden door was open so someone must be there. Sure enough, he heard a rattling of papers and footsteps coming toward him. He couldn't see anything inside the house because of the bright sunshine outside.

A man appeared in the doorway. He looked to be in his early fifties—tall and in good shape as though he took care of himself. His hair was a sandy red with a thick smattering of gray around his ears.

"Hello," the man said cordially. "May I help you?"

"Uh, yes." He waited a beat too long and added, "Please. I, uh, was looking for Lauren Mackenzie and was told that she was at this address."

The man stepped out onto the porch with Jordan, a forgotten paper clutched in his hand. The cordiality seemed to have slipped from his face unnoticed. He studied Jordan from the top of his head to the toes of his well-polished shoes. Jordan watched the man's jaw tighten as though he had clenched his teeth.

"You must be Jordan Trent," he said in a flat voice.

So much for impressing potential relatives.

Well, what the hell. Jordan grinned and stuck out his hand. "And you must be Matthew Mackenzie, the man my first son's going to be named after."

Matt looked at the hand held out to him and saw the capable strength there, as well as the hard austerity in the face and eyes that had seen too much of the wrong things of this world. Slowly changing the paper to his other hand Matt took the proffered hand and said, "In that case, perhaps you'd better come in."

Matt held the door open and Jordan stepped inside, feeling as though eyes were suddenly boring holes into his back.

The home exuded love, happiness and hospitality to such an extent that Jordan felt he could reach out and touch it. No wonder Lauren was the kind of woman she was—generously giving, warmhearted, and so wonderfully loving.

Jordan stood in the middle of the wide hallway and looked around. "Is Lauren here?"

"No."

The short word seemed to catch him in the midriff, winding him.

"Come on in and sit down," Matt said, waving to a front parlor that looked well lived in.

Jordan sat down across from the chair that had been occupied earlier by Lauren's father. Reading glasses lay nearby, as well as a tall glass of iced tea.

"May I get you something to drink?" Matt asked politely, noticing the direction of Jordan's eyes. The man certainly didn't miss much.

"No, thank you." Jordan waited until Matt sat down. "How did you know who I was?" he asked bluntly.

Matt tilted his head, still studying Jordan as though he were a microscopic specimen under a magnifying glass. "Lauren mentioned meeting a man of your description while she was in California a few weeks ago."

"I see." He looked around the room, trying to ignore the intent stare. Forcing his gaze back to the man across from him, he said, "What else did she have to say about me?"

"Very little."

"And from that you've decided you don't like me," Jordan stated flatly.

"I have no idea what I think about you personally. All I know is that when Lauren came home she was not the same person we've known for the past twenty-five years. Something had changed her. From the way her voice and facial expressions changed whenever she mentioned your name, I have a strong hunch that you had something to do with that change."

Jordan wished he could look on that information as positive, but it was too equivocal.

"I would really like to see your daughter, Mr. Mackenzie," Jordan said in a husky voice.

"Why?"

"I want to marry her," he stated baldly.

"Why?" Matt asked once more.

"Why?" Jordan repeated, puzzled. The answer seemed obvious. "Because I can't even think about a future that doesn't include her in it." His answer was as honest as he knew how to make it.

Matt's face seemed to soften for a moment. "You seem to have all the right answers. Does Lauren know how you feel?"

"I have no idea. That's why I'm here. I tried to contact her at work, but they said she—"

"Yes. She's taken a leave of absence."

"Is there something wrong? Has she been ill or something?"

He heard voices coming from the back of the house and glanced around. Feminine voices carrying on an animated conversation came closer down the hallway toward them. Jordan got to his feet because he recognized one of those voices. He would have recognized it anywhere, speaking any language.

Lauren and a woman who was obviously her mother appeared in the widely arched doorway. Lauren said, "We found your very favorite dessert at the bakery, Dad. So you can forget about your waistline for one evening and—"

Her eyes rested on the man standing there gazing at her; the man she had never expected to see again.

Lauren looked shocked, as though an apparition had appeared suddenly before her.

Her dad rose and began to say, "Lauren—" at the same time she whispered "Jordan!" and crumpled into a faint.

Twelve

Jordan was at her side in two long strides and had scooped her up and laid her on a nearby sofa before either parent moved.

Unusually quick reflexes, Matt decided, watching the younger man.

Whatever reactions Jordan had expected from Lauren, swooning at his feet hadn't been one of them. Lauren was too strong a person, she'd been too willing to accept everything that happened and deal with it to let his sudden appearance shock her so. Unless there was something wrong with her.

"What's wrong with her?" His question echoed his thoughts. From his position beside her on the couch, he glanced around at her parents' stricken faces.

"She's fainted," her father offered. "She's been

doing a lot of that lately. Takes after her mother in that respect, I'm afraid.''

Her mother said, ''I'll go get some water for her.''

After her mother left, Jordan looked up at the older man. ''What's causing her to faint? Has she been to the doctor?'' he demanded as though he had every right to know.

''Yes. As a matter of fact, Lauren went to the doctor earlier this week, after we insisted. The doctor explained that she has a slight case of pregnancy she's going to have to work through, but he expects her to recover in seven months or so.''

''Lauren's pregnant,'' Jordan repeated in a hollow voice.

No wonder Matthew Mackenzie had treated him like a suspect in a rape case. As far as he knew, Jordan was. What in the world had Lauren told them?

He felt her stir beside him. ''Lauren? Are you all right, love? Did you bump your head when you fell?'' he asked, gently stroking the hair away from her forehead.

Her eyes fluttered open and she stared up at the familiar face so close to hers.

''I thought I was imagining you,'' she said faintly.

He took her hand in his and gently squeezed. ''Oh, I'm real all right.''

''How's your back? Did the doctor say—''

''The doctor said a lot of things, but what does he know? Why did you leave?''

She continued to take in the familiar planes and hollows of his beloved face. ''You didn't need me anymore so I—''

"I'll always need you, love. I thought you knew that."

Her eyes darted past him to where her father stood, watching the scene thoughtfully. Her mother came hurrying into the room. "Oh, Lauren, you gave us such a fright. Of all the silly things to pass on to one of my daughters, fainting at the drop of a hat everytime I was—"

"Mother! Uh, I'd like you to meet Jordan Trent. Jordan, this is my mother, Hilary Mackenzie."

Jordan refused to let go of Lauren's hand. He nodded his head and smiled at the worried-looking woman.

"Oh!" Hilary exclaimed, "so *you're* Jordan!" as though putting all the pieces together.

"Mother? Don't you need to start dinner? I know Dad must be starving."

Her mother smiled at her daughter's agitation. It would take a crowbar to separate that young man from Lauren; Hilary had no trouble seeing that. Whatever the problem that had occurred between them, there was obviously no lack of love there.

Of course she had recognized Lauren's symptoms as soon as Lauren had arrived home, long before the idea of an unexpected pregnancy had occurred to the rest of the members of the family circle. Lauren was in love. There was no mistaking it. But Lauren hadn't wanted to talk about him so Hilary had known they must have had a spat of some sort.

She leaned over and patted her daughter's cheek. "Of course, darling. I'll get started right away." She glanced at Jordan with a twinkle in her eye, exchanged a meaningful glance with Matt and said to Jordan, "Of course you're planning to stay here with us, aren't you, Jordan? There's no reason to look for a room when we have this large house."

Lauren pushed herself to a sitting position, saying, "Mother, we have no idea why Jordan is even here. There's no reason to suppose he wants to stay over—"

"I'd be delighted to accept your hospitality, Mrs. Mackenzie," he said, smoothly interrupting Lauren's protests. "I was hoping to be able to spend some time talking to Lauren."

"I'm sure you could use some help in the kitchen," Matt said to Hilary, gently steering her to the door. "We can always get acquainted with Jordan over dinner."

After the two departed, the room seemed to fill with unspoken words and emotions. Jordan studied Lauren's pale skin. She wasn't taking care of herself. If anything happened to her he didn't know how he could ever bear it.

Without saying a word he pulled her into his arms and held her tightly against him. There was nothing sexual about the embrace. He just needed to have her close to him. God, but he'd missed her so much.

"What are you doing here?" she finally managed to say.

"I came to find you."

"Why?"

Now that he'd met Matt Mackenzie, Jordan could better understand where Lauren had gotten her habit of plain speaking.

"Because it's hard to carry on a marriage long-distance."

"That's finished now."

"Not according to our government."

"But Mallory said—"

"Despite what Mallory would like to have all of us think, Mallory does not control all parts of the government."

"I know that, but—"

"You have a passport that clearly states you are my wife."

"Yes, I know, but Mallory said it was all right to—"

"To falsify records? Shame on Mallory, misleading you that way. You've committed a serious crime, you know."

She looked at him warily. "Want to put that into the plural? Illegally exiting a country isn't considered a misdemeanor, you know."

"Well, I'm willing to do whatever I can to save your good name."

"What are you talking about?"

"I want that passport to be accurate, Lauren. Marry me."

"Why?"

"Damn it! Why do you ask so many questions?" He stood and began to pace the floor, which reminded her very much of the day they had first met. Yes, this was the Jordan Trent she remembered. Lauren dropped her head to hide her smile.

"Why does any man ask a woman to marry him? Because I want you to be my wife, the mother of my children. I want to wake up every morning knowing that you're there beside me. I want to go to sleep every night with my arms around you!" He was almost shouting at her, he was so frustrated.

Lauren bit her bottom lip, hard, to keep from laughing out loud. Never had she heard of such an unromantic proposal in all her life, which was why she believed he was sincere. If Jordan Trent had approached her with suave, polished phrases she'd have been suspicious of his motives.

Here was the man she'd fallen in love with: arrogant, impatient, hot-tempered—"Jordan?"

He spun around and faced her, legs braced, hands on his hips. "What?" He almost flinched at the harshness he heard in his tone. He knew he wasn't handling this right, but damn, she could be the most mulish...stubborn...adorable woman.... "I'm sorry, Lauren," he said in a lower voice. "I didn't mean to yell at you."

"May I have that in writing, please?" she asked with a smile. "I have a feeling that's the first apology you've ever made."

How could he resist her? He sank down on the sofa beside her once more, this time pulling her into his lap. "You're going to marry me, aren't you?" he asked softly, then kissed her before she had an opportunity to reply.

His dreams in the hospital had been filled with her, his feverish brain capturing her time and again to soothe him until he was able to hold her once more. No dream could compare with the reality.

"Oh, darlin', I've missed you so damned much. Please don't ever do this to me again."

"What did I do?"

"Disappear. I'm going to be very possessive of you until I can believe my luck in finding you again. I'll be afraid to blink for fear I'll wake up and you'll be gone."

"I didn't mean to upset you by leaving."

"You did an excellent job of it."

"I thought it was better this way."

"For whom?"

"For both of us. After all, your life-style is so different. You never know where you're going to be from one week to the next—"

"Oh, yes, I do. Sitting behind Mallory's desk."

She leaned back in his arms and stared at him in shock. "What happened to Mallory?"

Jordan laughed. "Why? Did you think I did something to him?"

"No, seriously."

"Seriously, Mallory has been promoted. Therefore, so have I."

"But do you want to work behind a desk?"

"And spend my evenings with you? You're damned right. I'll never be much use around a house, but since I've touched very little of a very large salary over the years, we can always hire someone to keep the house repaired, do yard work and—"

Lauren stopped his speech by leaning over and kissing him gently on the mouth. That got his undivided attention. When at last she drew away from him, she said with amusement, "Just as long as you don't decide to hire someone to take your place in my bed."

"Then you're going to marry me?" he asked, afraid to allow himself to believe that despite everything, she was willing to take him on as a husband.

"Mallory's the one who first mentioned that you always got what you go after. I have a feeling I wouldn't have a prayer if I tried to resist."

The smile he gave her lit up the room. She was touched. He had absolutely no idea how she felt about him. Of course she'd never put it into words. She hadn't felt it necessary, any more than she felt the need to force him to admit that he loved her.

She might never hear him say it, but she didn't care. He had showed her in every way he was capable of demonstrating his feelings.

"When would you like to get married?" she asked, still sitting in his lap, her arms around his neck.

"Tomorrow."

"I'm not sure I could manage that."

"Well, the thing is, Mallory's finally going to let me have my vacation and I thought that Santiago Island might make a great place for a honeymoon. We could stay there until we get bored, then decide what we want to do next."

"Besides, you need to finish recuperating."

"I'm already feeling a hundred percent better." He glanced toward the open doorway. "By the way, what did you tell your dad about me? He mentioned that you told him we met in California."

"Since that's where I'm supposed to have been, where else would I have met you?"

"He treated me like a professional seducer of innocent maidens."

Lauren's cheeks turned a rosy hue. "Fathers are kinda like that," she murmured. "Protective of their daughters."

Jordan saw the little red-headed girl in his mind once again, and knew that he would be just as bad, if not worse.

"I'm sorry if I've ever caused you any pain, Lauren. I've never wanted to hurt you."

"You haven't. Not really. It's just that I could never see how we could work it out so we could spend our lives together."

"But we can. And we have." He waited for her to tell him about the pregnancy. He didn't want her to know that he already knew. He didn't want to take any chances on her thinking that was the reason he'd proposed. Her dad had known differently. Jordan had announced his intentions before he'd ever learned about her condition.

Nuzzling her neck, he asked, "Are you planning to go back to work?"

She became still in his arms and he waited, nibbling on her earlobe. "Would you like me to?"

He smiled, but she couldn't see his amusement. "I want you to do whatever you want to do, darlin'." He waited, almost holding his breath.

"Well, I'm not really sure what to do at the moment."

"Then let's play it by ear, okay? Just know that whatever you decide is fine with me."

He could feel her slowly relaxing against him. So she wasn't ready to tell him. It made no difference to him. Jordan was rather pleased with the timing of everything. If she weren't already pregnant she might have insisted that they wait and get to know each other better. Or she might have decided that she didn't want to marry him at all.

The first thing he intended to do upon the arrival of his son or daughter was to thank him or her for helping him accomplish the most important assignment of his career.

Epilogue

Sparkling white sand glinted like diamonds in the sunlight. Turquoise-blue water looked so artificial that Lauren was convinced the natives must sneak out at night after all the tourists were asleep and pour bluing into the lagoon.

They had been on the island for three wonderful days and exciting nights. Jordan had insisted that she keep a strong sun block on her skin. He loved the ivory tone and wanted nothing to harm it. Consequently, they only swam early in the morning and in the late evening, after the sun's rays had lessened.

Now they were stretched out side by side in the shade of their palm-thatched porch, lazily watching the soft rhythm of the waves and the swaying palm trees.

"This is a far cry from Czechoslovakia," Lauren murmured as though to herself.

They shared a double lounger. Jordan opened one eye and looked over at her skimpily-clad body. He was glad he'd been able to rent this small cabana away from everything else on the island. Initially he'd wanted the privacy for resting when he'd been here on his own. Now he wanted the privacy to keep everyone from enjoying his wife's rather delectable form, particularly in the evening when he coaxed her to go skinny-dipping with him.

"Oh, I don't know," he said, lazily dropping his hand onto her bare midriff. "I've noticed that there are some basic similarities."

"Such as?"

"We seem to spend a great deal of our time in bed together."

"Well, that beats getting shot at."

"I'm glad you think so. Otherwise I might have worried about my technique."

The sound she made could only be likened to a rather ladylike snort. "You're too arrogant to worry over anything you do. You think you're perfect."

"Hardly."

"I have to admit you manage to come very close at times."

He turned over and kissed her along the edge of her bikini top. "For instance?"

"If you think I'm going to lie here extolling your virtues and give you more reason to be obnoxiously arrogant, you're crazy."

"That's what I love about you, woman—all of those affectionate endearments that just roll off your lips." His hand slid beneath the thin top and he cupped her full breast, gently rubbing his thumb over the nipple. Did she think he hadn't noticed that her breasts had become fuller in the last several weeks?

She took a quick breath at his touch and he hid his smile by nudging the offending cloth out of the way and placing his lips around the tip of her breast.

Lauren ran her hands through his hair, holding him close. She had never imagined that her life could turn out so perfectly. Jordan seemed to be content just being with her. The tense professional had disappeared. In his place a teasing, boyish, passionate man had appeared. She loved his playful mood. In fact she loved everything about him... his openness with her, his complete honesty... which was why she was having such a tough time figuring out how to tell him that she was pregnant.

It wasn't the sort of thing she could drop into a casual conversation. Not that she had meant to keep the news a secret from him, not after he'd shown up at her parents' home.

Before then there had been some poignant discussions with her mother and dad who had felt he had a right to know about the baby. She hadn't seen it that way. He'd already made it clear how he felt about children, and his professional life was totally incompatible with any normal family life.

His unexpected appearance had changed all of that. He'd obviously come looking for her in order to demand that she marry him. She grinned at the thought.

Never once had he asked her how she felt about getting married. He'd been just like her father, taking it for granted.

Lauren's thoughts scattered into fragments of disconnected images as Jordan finished removing her top and reached down to slide his hand inside the bottom half. He gently rubbed her skin so that all she could think about was Jordan and how he made her feel.

He never seemed to get enough of touching her, even when he had no intention of making love to her. Wherever they were, whatever they did, he either held her hand or touched her arm or kept his hand on the small of her back.

Lauren had discovered a definite indication in herself that touching him could become addictive as well. He had turned a deep golden brown since they'd arrived on the beach. And why not? He spent most of his time in the sun while insisting she stay protected from the harsh rays. The swimsuit he wore did absolutely nothing to conceal his masculinity. If anything it emphasized how well endowed he was.

His mouth gently pressed kisses across her stomach, down and across her abdomen, down and down—"Jordan!" she gasped.

"I know, love. Just relax and let me love you." He had taken all kinds of liberties with her, teaching her variations of lovemaking that had sent her spiraling over the edge time and again and he'd discovered several ways to make her wild with passion. He seemed to enjoy bringing out that fierce response in her.

Lauren couldn't lie still. She wanted to touch him, to love him, to express to him all that she couldn't find the words to say. By the time he stretched out over her she was sobbing with the need to love him.

He took her in one powerful surge, lifting her so that her thighs locked tightly around him. She clung to him, wordlessly pleading for release, her soft, incoherent moans and gasps sending him into an orbit of pleasure, knowing that he was able to give her so much pleasure in return.

They were oblivious to the day, the glistening sand, the turquoise-blue water, the swaying palm trees. The view was wasted but neither one cared.

Jordan kept the pace relentlessly rhythmical until Lauren cried out, her voice sounding like one of the gulls that visited their stretch of beach from time to time. Only then did he allow himself his own release. He gave one final, convulsive lunge, grasping her so closely that she could barely get her breath.

She didn't care.

He rolled, carrying her with him so that their positions were reversed on the wide lounger. She lay limply sprawled across his body, her head pillowed on his chest. His lungs still labored to get enough oxygen to his body.

"Jordan?" He felt her tense slightly.

"Hmmmm," he responded drowsily.

"You know, we haven't been using anything to prevent a pregnancy..."

He tried not to make any moves that would alert her to his reaction to the conversation.

"That's true," he said lazily, running his hand through her hair.

"You once said you didn't want children," she tentatively offered.

"I did? Must have been out of my mind. I love children. We've got to have at least two, one of each." He could feel her body began to relax once again.

"I'd like that," she said softly. After a few minutes of silence she said, "Of course you probably aren't all that anxious to start on a family right away..." she trailed off, wishing she knew how to just starkly tell him that, like it or not, he was going to be a father in a little more than six months! Lauren had never before considered herself a coward. But she was. Oh, yes, indeed. And she was proving it with every evasion she uttered.

Jordan could feel her apprehension and wished he knew how to help her. At this point in their relationship it wouldn't help her to know that he'd discovered her condition after she'd fainted. Someday... maybe...he might tell her. But for the time being he'd made Matt Mackenzie swear to secrecy.

"Oh, I don't know," he said. "I'm not getting any younger. I think it would be rather nice to have our children early, give them a chance to have as young parents as possible and—"

"Oh, Jordan, do you really mean that?" she asked, raising her head and looking at him for the first time in several minutes.

"Yes, darling. I really mean it. I love you and I'll love our children. You are the world to me."

Tears glistened in her eyes. "That's the first time you've ever told me you love me, did you know that?"

He raised his head slightly and kissed her swollen, well-loved mouth. "I've told you I loved you with everything I've done and said since I first met you. I just didn't know it at the time."

He waited expectantly, aware of her search for the words to tell him about the baby. He had so many questions he wanted to ask about the whole birthing process.

Would she want him with her at the time of birth? If not, he'd just have to spend the next few months convincing her that he was just as indispensable at the delivery as he was at the conception. He smiled, already knowing what she would have to say about his arrogance.

"Uh, Jordan, I think there's something you should know," Lauren began with a tentative smile.

*   *   *   *   *

BY DEBBIE MACOMBER....

ONCE UPON A TIME, in a land not so far away, there lived a girl, Debbie Macomber, who grew up dreaming of castles, white knights and princes on fiery steeds. Her family was an ordinary one with a mother and father and one wicked brother, who sold copies of her diary to all the boys in her junior high class.

One day, when Debbie was only nineteen, a handsome electrician drove by in a shiny black convertible. Now Debbie knew a prince when she saw one, and before long they lived in a two-bedroom cottage surrounded by a white picket fence.

As often happens when a damsel fair meets her prince charming, children followed, and soon the two-bedroom cottage became a four-bedroom castle. The kingdom flourished and prospered, and between soccer games and car pools, ballet classes and clarinet lessons, Debbie thought about love and enchantment and the magic of romance.

One day Debbie said, "What this country needs is a good fairy tale." She remembered how well her diary had sold and she dreamed again of castles, white knights and princes on fiery steeds. And so the stories of Cinderella, Beauty and the Beast, and Snow White were reborn....

Look for Debbie Macomber's *Legendary Lovers* trilogy from Silhouette Romance: *Cindy and the Prince* (January, 1988); *Some Kind of Wonderful* (March, 1988); *Almost Paradise* (May, 1988). Don't miss them!

SRT-1

 **Silhouette Desire**

COMING
NEXT MONTH

#415 FEVER—Elizabeth Lowell
World traveler Lisa Johansen had never met a man like Ryan McCall
before. Their love grew in a sweet summer meadow, but would the
bond between them be broken when Rye revealed his
true identity?

#416 FOR LOVE ALONE—Lucy Gordon
His new bride woke, remembering nothing, and Corrado Bennoni
was glad. Fate had given him a second chance to win Philippa...for
love alone.

#417 UNDER COVER—Donna Carlisle
Detective Teale Saunders saw an innate honesty beneath con man
David Carey's polished facade. When she fell in love with the man
she was duty-bound to arrest, she learned that things aren't always
black or white.

#418 NO TURNING BACK—Christine Rimmer
Jake Strand had seen her at the worst of times, and Caitlin O'Neill
wanted no part of him. But for Jake she had been his turning point,
and his hope for the future lay with her.

#419 THE SECOND MR. SULLIVAN—Elaine Camp
Notorious Beau Sullivan wasn't at all like Kelly had expected—and
when he started to romance her, she found her ex-brother-in-law hard
to resist!

#420 ENAMORED—Diana Palmer
Neither Melissa Sterling nor Diego Laremos was able to resist their
passion in the steamy Guatemalan jungle. Torn apart by their
families' past, they had to learn trust before they could
be reunited.
